D0961834

RONAN BOYLE

INTO·THE·

STRANGEPLACE

RONAN

·INTO·THE·

AMULET BOOKS

NEW YORK

BOYLE

STR▲NGEPLACE

THOMAS LENNON

·ILLUSTRATED BY JOHN HENDRIX·

Cataloging-in-Publication Data has been applied for and may be obtained from the Library of Congress.

ISBN 978-1-4197-5330-5

Text copyright © 2021 Thomas Lennon
Illustrations copyright © 2021 John Hendrix
Book design by Hana Anouk Nakamura
Original book design by Chad W. Beckerman

Printed and bound in U.S.A.
10 9 8 7 6 5 4 3 2 1

Amulet Books are available at special discounts when purchased in quantity for premiums and promotions as well as fundraising or educational use. Special editions can also be created to specification. For details, contact specialsales@abramsbooks.com or the address below.

Amulet Books® is a registered trademark of Harry N. Abrams, Inc.

ABRAMS The Art of Books
195 Broadway, New York, NY 10007
abramsbooks.com

For Michelle McNamara,
my friend who went on ahead to scout Tir na Nog

RONAN BOYLE

·INTO·THE·

STRANGEPLACE

Chapter One
EASY STREET

In their homeland that the leprechauns call Tir na Nog, darkness came as softly as someone flipping up your hoodie.

My partner, Lily, a rust-colored wolfhound, was at my side. She shook off the last dampness of the River of GLOOM, which we left in our wake. Lily is the size of a Shetland pony, but ten times more lovable. We had passed into in the Place that Smells Like Feet, which I had just named for reasons that are obvious.

There is no sense of time in the land of the faerie folk. The wee folk just call every day "Nonsday." I looked up and saw that the sky was full of the leprechaun constellations—as it was what we would call nighttime back in the Human Republic of Ireland.

Tir na Nog is its own dominion, with its own weather systems, and even its own laws of physics. For example, in the clurichaun towns called the Floating Lakes, the gravitational pull is up. The residents have gotten used to it, but it makes the few humans who have visited barf, which is the non-Scottish word for *boke*.

Tir na Nog has its own firmament of stars that has no relation to human astrology (Orion the Hunter, the Big Dipper, and all those classics). Under the violent leprechaun's separatist Queen Moira with the World's Most Interesting Forehead, the leprechauns rearranged their constellations into shapes that they find hilarious.

The leprechaun sense of humor is depraved. Major figures in their night sky are: Unicorn Picking Its Nose, Queen Moira Ripping a Humongous Toot, and the one by which sailors in the Leprechaun Royal Navy steer their ships: Somebody's Butt with an Eyeball in the Crack, sometimes called Cyclops Eyeball-Butt.

Leprechauns are the worst.

I stopped to check my bootlaces, which were tangled like those garlic bulb thingies that hang in Italian restaurants. During the past few stressful days in North Ifreann, I had been nervously adding knot upon knot to my Special Unit boots, which are designed to withstand the bite of a medium-power leprechaun. It would take a brain surgeon to cut me out of these.

Lily and I were headed toward something called The Very Short Cut, which leads from the Undernog all the way to the lower slopes of the Unpronounceable Volcano, which is just a few day's journey DownNog from the seat of the Leprechaun Royal Family: Oifigtown (SEE MAP).

TIR·NA·NOG

SHENANOGRAM

In a vastsack in my sporran was a team of weegees, the corrupt leprechaun police force. (A vastsack is a Special Unit evidence bag that has a huge interior compartment but is tiny on the outside. This one looked like a Roscommon Football Club souvenir coin purse.)

In my vastsack with the weegees was an old Irish god called Crom Cruach, who I had turned from "alive" to "no longer alive" with a terrific poke in the heart from my very nice umbrella.

My mission was to turn over these corrupt wee folk to the leprechaun king who resides in the royal palace in Oifigtown, the capital of Tir na Nog. I have never met a leprechaun royal (or even a human royal, except for the guy in Galway who calls himself the "King of Hassle-Free Mobile Phones"). Upon closing this case, I would then return to the Human Republic of Ireland with Crom Cruach the no-longer-alive bog mummy, where he could be safely encased in the National Museum, Dublin, and perhaps the plaque beside his case would make some mention of the clever boy Ronan Boyle who brought him to justice with the help of Lily the world's bravest wolfhound.

My parents had been framed for the theft of the Bog Man by a pointy art dealer known as Lord Desmond Dooley. But they had recently escaped the Mountjoy Prison along with their prison gangs—*which I had said was a bad idea at the time.* My parents are museum types, but when you fall in with a prison gang like they did, you're definitely going to get peer pressured.

Currently, my parents' whereabouts are unknown. I don't like to use the word *escapees*, as it looks bad on their résumés, but technically that is exactly what they are.

My unofficial mentor and occasional partner, Captain de Valera, was recovering back at Special Unit headquarters in Killarney after our violent dustup in North Ifreann. So Lily and I were on our own, for now, but I could feel that we were in the home stretch!

Just a quick little jaunt through this famous short cut and easy-peasy, I'd be sitting back at Dough Bros. pizza in Galway, telling this whole affair to Dolores, my hilarious guardian and the best rockabilly fiddle player you will meet in the Human Republic of Ireland.

Compared to the mayhem back in North Ifreann, this next bit was going to be a lark.

Chapter Two
LAURA THE CAVE WHALE

The Very Short Cut is labeled on all Special Unit maps. At fifteen years old, I am the youngest person ever to hold the rank of detective in the organization, which means I get the privilege to carry one of these coveted maps, and I only had to pay 75 euros for it plus tax.

What's *not* on the map is a description of how the Short Cut works, which I was about to learn the disgusting way. The Short Cut is nestled in a putrid cavern, 3 kilometers from the River of GLOOM and stretches a kilometer into the ground. The temperature in the cave is 45 degrees

Celsius, which in Fahrenheit would be something like 113, or the hottest temperatures at which a human can briefly survive, while getting some brain damage.

No ordinary creature can live permanently under these conditions, and I assure you, the creature who lives here is far from ordinary.

The human realm has seventy-six kinds of whales with teeth. The faerie realm has three more than that. The bonus whales of the faerie realm include The Hoof-less Narwhal (a thirty-ton, sea-based unicorn that feeds on whole villages of merrows in one lunch break), the Left Whale (opposite of a Right Whale; can play guitar upside down in the style of the famous human Jimi Hendrix of Seattle, Washington, USA), and the largest and most unsightly specimen of omnivorous nonfiction whale: The Cave Whale.

We had been corkscrewing down into the cave for about a human hour, getting mild brain damage and hanging on to the sizzling stalagmites that lined this nightmarish route. Just when things couldn't get more unpleasant—we met Laura.

Laura the Cave Whale is the most inaccurately named creature that I've crossed paths with. When I hear the word *Laura*, I think of a freckle-faced human doing chores for ma and pa instead of a nightmarish super-slug the length and girth of four London Underground train cars.

Inaptly named Laura is covered in gelatinous spikes, which secrete a mucus that protects her from the heat. It smells like inexpensive pad Thai that somebody put extra shrimp powder in without telling the recipient, who might be very allergic to it.

Laura's maw is wide enough to inhale all of Manchester United (thirty-seven-ish persons at the time of my writing this). Her underbite shows off a set of rotten fangs that resembles the Tokyo skyline after a successful Mothra attack. Her emerald-colored eyes are huge, but purely decorative, as seven hundred years in a cave has left her legally blind. Some reports say that if you linger too long in the lair of Laura, she will force you to read all of the small print on her prescription bottles.

Laura undulated herself toward us in a squishy way that

would remind anyone of a caterpillar that happened to be the size of a London Bakerloo Line train.

"Who dares to enter the cave of Laura and ruin the vibe with their horrible aura?" bellowed the cave whale, inflating herself like a whoopee cushion and spraying Lily and me with a few hundred liters of hot whale mucus.

"Um. Hello, madame whale. Ronan Boyle here, come to your cave, looking for a bit of time to save," I said, wiping mucus off my neck and taking her cue and speaking in rhyme, which is considered polite in those parts of Tir na Nog where the creatures speak. (Technically, Laura was what Special Unit handbooks would classify as monster, not creature.)

"If yer looking to make some haste, then roll in the truffle salt and let's see how you taste," said Laura, blinking her giant useless eyes and nodding toward a nearby lagoon of truffle-salted water that bubbled and burped.

I looked to Lily to see if she understood this exchange as I had. Lily nodded. Apparently we were to roll ourselves in this little salt lake and *feed ourselves to her*? Yech. This is why I've never liked Wednesdays.

> *Just to be clear,*
>
> *madame, it appears,*
>
> *we must go in your gut*
>
> *to use the short cut?*

I stammered, trying to not let the whale mucus drip from my nose into my mouth and . . . UGH. FAIL. THERE IT GOES. IT HAPPENED. WHALE MUCUS RIGHT INTO MY MOUTH.

> *Indeed, narrow human,*
>
> *ye must get consumed, then*
>
> *you'll travel quite fast,*
>
> *through my stomach you'll pass,*
>
> *then launch from my blowhole right into the air,*
>
> *it's all a tasty and painless affair,*
>
> *and I should point out, for it's known near and far,*
>
> *if you enjoy Laura's service—please use the tip jar,*

Said the cave whale, her snout wriggling a bit toward an old jar half-filled with euros, harps, and faerie gold.

I fumbled into my sporran, found a 5-euro note, and crammed it into the jar, folding it in a way that made it seem like *two* 5-euro notes, a trick I learned from Dolores Mullen, my human guardian back in Galway.

Lily and I flopped around a bit in the truffle salt lake, which to my surprise was an absolute delight. The density of the salt water makes mammals like Lily and me float with a zippy feeling of weightlessness. If not for the pizza-oven temperature in the cave that was permanently damaging my brain, I would have lingered on the surface there for some time, but Laura sniffed at us with her strange concave nose. She seemed to think we had been marinated enough, and she sucked us into her terrifying maw with a mighty slurp.

Scientists would describe the next bit as "icky." We spun about in Laura's mouth while she gummed at us. She didn't use her teeth, just savored us, the same way you might quietly keep a caramel in your mouth during a play. I clung onto Lily for dear life. In my mind I was being dragged back to a very specific horror from my past—a fateful Saturday in the second grade, when Kevin Farrell's bouncy castle popped, leaving my classmates and me trapped and flailing—a panicked pile of pizza-stuffed children.

As I was starting to black out from post-traumatic bouncy castle stress, an undertow pulled us into Laura's esophagus, forcing us into something that was either her stomach or lungs. With a rush of hot wind, we were burped from her blowhole like living whale snot.

Chapter Three
THE UNPRONOUNCEABLE VOLCANO

Lily and I were about 90 meters in the air, looking down over a jagged facade of lava rock.

It was a balmy day in the air above the volcano with a name that nobody can pronounce. Technically it's written in the faerie-folk version of a font that is the equivalent to the human one known as Zapf Dingbats. Written down, it looks something like this:

★☆✠✤ ★★✳ ★★★★★✩✩★ ✢✳✠✢★✠✳

Frizzy vapor wafted from the volcano's caldera, which I

think is what you call the opening part of a volcano or is the name of a heavy metal band from Norway.

Falling 90 meters onto rock candy looked like it would really hurt, and one second later, this proved to be super true!

My landing felt like someone shuffling the discs of my spine for a new round of *Let's Kill Ronan Boyle*. Then, I did the thing that I am probably better at than anyone you know: I shrieked like a parrot who had just stumbled on the scene of a triple homicide.

The Unpronounceable Volcano lies in a disputed area between Dun Gollie (the beautiful gancanagh capital) and Oifigtown (the mischievous leprechaun capital and their financial headquarters). Tragically, these two kinds of wee folk have been in a feud over this area for thirty-five thousand human years, or what to them feels like last April.

The volcano is considered valuable, as it pumps out a rare sparkling white wine, which cannot be called *Champagne* as it's not from that region of France. But it looks and smells exactly like Champagne. Tragically, lots of wee-tourists are lost into the Unpronounceable Volcano on a daily basis, often with the entire motor coach they were traveling in. As with all of the minutiae about the wee folk, it should be noted that they don't even like the taste of Champagne. After they drink Champagne they get horrible headaches and end up facedown in a pile of coats.

In my training back at Collins House, it was explained that the dispute over the Unpronounceable Champagne Volcano works as follows: WHILE NEITHER SIDE LIKES THE TASTE OF THE CHAMPAGNE VOLCANO, THEY DO NOT WANT THE OTHER SIDE TO HAVE IT.

So, both sides *pretend* to like Champagne, and have fought a war for thirty-five thousand years. This makes sense to leprechauns.

Dazed from the hard landing, Lily and I limped our way along the slope until we came upon the thing on my map called The Decent Restaurant. The only part about The Decent Restaurant that wasn't really true was the middle part.

The place is cozy enough—a little thatched roof

establishment with a central fireplace like an old black-smith's shop. A stuffed unicorn head was mounted above the cash register, which you and I might find horrifying, but is less distressing, as these "trophies" are almost always fakes, available mail-order from North Ifreann.

Lily and I both had pressed sandwiches made labo-riously by the chef, a far darrig with two heads named FinneganAndAlsoDonovan.

Not complaining—but what is the point of a two-headed far darrig, when it takes them thirty human minutes to make *two* sandwiches? I would put all of this in my two-star review later, in the Special Unit of Tir na Nog APP, which has been glitchy lately.

"How's your taco-that-got-rained-on sandwich treat-ing you?" FinneganAndAlsoDonovan's left head asked Lily. (They had made her sandwich in a wolfhound flavor.) Lily nodded and made convincing yummy growls, and if you did not know her, you certainly would have thought that she was having the time of her life.

As our sandwiches settled, Lily and I consulted my

map and plotted a route to Oifigtown. My plan was to head toward the coast, then hug along the shoreline up to the royal seat. This would help us to stay out of the Left Unknown, which is a place about which little is known. Considering the terrifying things we humans do know about Tir Na Nog, I was looking forward to skipping this vague area.

FinneganAndAlsoDonovan's right head gave us directions along with the bill for lunch that was the absurd price of 80 euros or one leprechaun harp. Since we were traveling harp-less, I paid them with the very last European currency I had in my sporran. I resisted the urge to check inside my vastsack and see what mischief my prisoners were up to in there. A general Special Unit rule is once you have put arrestees into a sack, don't open it until you have backup! WHEN YOU OPEN THAT SACK, PREPARE FOR ATTACK! is a poster on the wall in the Supply and Weapons Department at Collins House, the Special Unit Headquarters back in Killarney.

I thought for a long moment about Captain de Valera,

my mentor and friend and superior officer and whatnot. I tried *not* to remember the bit about me shouting out that I was in love with her back in North Ifreann, when I stole her back from the undead Bog Man. That was just a heat-of-the-moment type of slipup. In truth: I don't think I am in love with the captain. I have never been in love; why should I be now at just the age of fifteen, when people are least likely to fall in love? Isn't it more logical that sometimes you have a friend and you enjoy the way they smell so much that you seek it out and their face seems like some kind of magic trick that keeps happening and never gets old no matter how many times you see it? And then also one day you accidentally see their shoulder blades and you wonder how they became so perfect, like the neck of a cello made by the angels in heaven?

That's just regular ol' friendship in my book!

And this terribly ordinary and stupid boring feeling is what I have about Captain de Valera. PFFT. NOTHING TO WRITE HOME ABOUT.

If I were romantically in love with the captain, WHO IS FIVE (ISH) years older than me (UGH!!!! GROSS.

YECCHHHHHHH. BARF AND/OR BOKE, AS GARY THE WEREWOLF WOULD SAY.), if I were in love with her, I would say the kind of dumb mushy things that gross old people in love say, like "Should we go have fish-and-chips tonight, dear?" or similar rubbish. I would never say something like that to the captain, as she is very imposing. The only adult who intimidates me more than the captain is Yogi Hansra, my shillelagh combat teacher and the human world's best shillelagh fighter.

Lily's super nose picked up a scent as we leaped off of the last bit of the sticky volcano down toward the area of sparkling white wine hot springs that puddles up at the gancanagh side of the Unpronounceable Volcano.

There were once wall-to-wall gancanagh hotels on the slope of the volcano. While they despise the taste of the sparkling hot springs, they do like how the springs feel on their backsides, feet, and inside their ear passages. The gancanaghs use the hot springs to clean out their various cracks and crevices.

Due to the thirty-five thousand years of war, there's only really one good hotel still open down here: L'Orangerie. L'Orangerie looks more like a fortress than a resort. The facade has been sandbagged and wrapped with razor wire. In sprawling graffiti across the front, someone has sprayed: YOU CAN'T KILL THE LEPRECHAUNS! But just below that, in gancanagh script, someone added: UNLESS WE ALL WORK TOGETHER!

Within sniffing distance of L'Orangerie, I pulled my beret down over my eyes and rode on Lily's back. Gancanagh folk are so astonishingly beautiful that upon seeing one of them, a human will fall instantly in love and give them everything they own: jewelry, glass eye, the toupee off their skull. A gancanagh spell was not a risk I could take right now, so close to the completion of this mission.

In the darkness of my optional beret, I heard Lily exchange words with a few gancanaghs, and even their voices were pleasing to my ears. So pleasing. Perhaps I should give them this beret? NO!

Lily trotted along with me as cargo for a "spell," which

is one of the only human measures of time that wee folk understand (a "spell" is seventy-two human minutes). I could make out the sounds of exploding EYEBROW-REMOVING DEVICES dangerously close at hand. E.R.D.s are a weapon I had never even heard about in training. Leprechauns invented Eyebrow-Removing Devices to battle gancanaghs in this pointless, stupid war. The depths to which the wee folk will go to inflict harm on their own kind is rivaled only by that of humans.

An Eyebrow Removing Device works like this (sensitive readers should skip this bit.):

In what humans would think of as 2500 BCE, or the time of the building of the pyramids—or what the wee folk would call "two Nonsdays ago—the leprechauns discovered that they could *catch* a hot pickle fart from their bottom and seal it up inside a glass jar. (This could only be done if they were farting like lightning, and had two nonjudgmental friends to help them get the lid on.)

Then they would leave this horrid jar of farts in the sun, letting it mature like some poisonous wine. After a thousand years or so, that pickle toot in a jar becomes wea-ponized. It transforms into the foulest smelling thing in the universe. Not just on planet earth, not just in Tir na Nog—the worst smelling thing in all of space and time, which holds as many suns as there are grains of sand and may be expanding at a rate that we can never measure or even understand. This fact has been corroborated by the European Space Agency (which is probably the top space agency located in downtown Paris).

You may be wondering: *Ronan Boyle, who has time to fart in so many jars and keep them around? Don't leprechauns have better things to do with their time?*

Not really, no.

Everything UpNog of L'Orangerie Hotel is an active war zone. It's where the gorgeous gancanagh forces clash with tiny, stinky leprechauns on a daily basis in a fetid wasteland of broken E.R.D.s and solid gold arrows. Golden arrows are the gancanagh projectile of choice, and while they look fantastic, they're way too heavy to get more than a few meters. If a gancanagh ever aims a golden arrow at you, don't even stress. Unless you're in the town of the Floating Lakes, or literally standing right next to them, you'll be fine.

I could hear gancanagh forces patrolling while riding on geleflocks, which are creatures that look like an ostrich, but with the face of someone's annoyed aunt.

When Lily's pads were tender from the journey, we traded places and I carried her on my back, which I am able to do in bursts of up to almost a minute.

At dusk, the constellation Cyclops Eyeball-Butt was rising in the sky. We had limped all the way to the South coast of Tir na Nog, where the Sea of Uiscecúr churns against the mainland, blasting pink foam a kilometer into the air.

I cut the laces off of my boots with the sock knife that goes with the Special Unit kilt and cost me 80 euros. (At this point I was almost 750 euros in debt to the Special Unit. Still, it's a fun job, and I don't want to discourage you from enlisting!)

I wriggled my toes, which resemble my face more than you would imagine, into the fine black sand. Lily did the same with her pads, digging about like a wild dingo before she settled, which wolfhounds will always do by instinct, no matter how many generations they have lived indoors.

The Sea of Uiscecúr is sweet rather than salty, and my feet would remain sticky and watermelon-scented for several spells. Along the shoreline of Tir na Nog are carved ancient emerald totems of the old gods. Like the Easter Island heads of the human realm, these massive stone faces look out at the sea and offer protection, or perhaps a warning to travelers. The faces I could (vaguely) recognize were: a giant with one eyeball, a friendly cow, a naked lady on a horse, an angry lady with a harp, and the only one I recognized for sure: Crom Cruach.* Yes—one and the same. The undead god of child-eating that was tied up in the sack on my belt. The carving of his face was so accurate, it looked like he had posed for this sculpture himself. Perhaps he did sit for it, as it looked to be his twin, age wise.

I wriggled myself into the cozy sand nest that Lily had dug for us and watched the leprechaun constellation Grandma Falls Off Riding Mower move across the heavens.

At daybreak, I hoped that we would make our way up

---

*Hello! Your associate Finbar Dowd, Deputy Commissioner of the Special Unit, here with my longest footnote to date, which means 99 percent of you will skip it. Ah well, such is my lot in life, and perhaps it's why I am such a catch on paper, but unmarried in real life, living in a flat in Killarney with Chef Gregor from the wonderful Collins House Cafeteria and playing bit parts in community theater. Detective Boyle has not read much ancient Irish history or he would know these stone famous figures are clearly:

—BALOR, nasty Celtic god and giant with a singular eye, standing with his friend . . .

the coastline and make sight of Oifigtown within two or three lunchtimes.

This, of course, was just the plan. And like they say: Everyone has a plan until they get smacked in the face.

Lily and I were about to get smacked.

—GLAS GAIBHNENN, a magical cow that made so much more milk than other cows that it was considered magic! Imagine that? That's beaucoup de milk! Please note that the magic Irish cow of ancient times is not affiliated with Donn Cúailnge, the magical bull of ancient times. NO RELATION. Also Donn Cúailnge predates by four thousand years the magical Chicago Bull known as Michael Jordan, who is related to the flying faerie folk on his great-grandmother's side, which (SPOILER ALERT) explains the 1988 All Star Slam Dunk Contest.
—CANOLA is the serious lady with the harp, Irish goddess of music with the name spelled just like the cooking oil. She made her first harp from the bones and ripped-out tendons of a dead whale (fun and true!).
—Look out, EPONA is that young starlet on the horse! And she's not just the god of horses, but donkeys as well! If you ever see donkeys praying with heads down, they're probably singing little songs about Epona! Rumor has it that unicorns were originally just a group of disgruntled horses that tried to weaponize their heads with old seashells. They planned to murder Epona in around seven thousand BCE. Epona and her followers were mightier in battle and vanquished the unicorns, who turned into the surly, gossipy, violent creatures we know today.
Phew. End of my footnote!

See you soon, your man in Killarney, F.D.

Chapter Four
THE WEE FREAKS OF THE SEA

The sound of a deranged orchestra tuning up should have been taken as a warning. I was snuggling beneath Lily in the black sand, feeling cozy and warm for the first time in ages, licking a bit of watermelon sea breeze off of my lips, when the strains of a fiddle and oboe cut their way through the crash of the sea foam.

I rolled to my side and pushed lightly on the sides of my eyeballs—a little trick I do when I am too lazy to put on my glasses. I'm not sure exactly how it works, but it seems to change the shape of the rods or cones and I can see sharply for a moment, like do-it-yourself LASIK surgery.

A leprechaun galleon flying battle flags and the Standard of the Leprechaun Royal Family was dropping anchor just beyond the breakwater. While the orchestra vamped on the foredeck of the ship, down the starboard side, a longboat of colorful wee folk was being lowered down. The wee folk were dancing with SO MUCH enthusiasm.

The wee folk in the longboat were dressed in multicolored leotards and jazz shoes. They rowed toward shore at a brisk pace, but also, while some rowed, others pretended to row, in pantomime. Why? I cannot say.

Their movements were choreographed, and honestly, way over the top.

The wee sailors were performing a musical number that needed a ton of work. While I was not able to remember it verbatim, it went like this, accompanied by sparkle fingers and unnecessary gyrations:

> *Here comes the Wee Navy,*
> *Shaking your fruit tree,*
> *Got too dry on land,*

So we get freaky at sea.

We rock in the day,

And freak you at night,

We wear character shoes,

With nondescript tights.

We sing o'er the waves,

Paying our dues,

We give it our all,

Just don't read the reviews.

(all, trying to harmonize)

DON'T READ THE REVIEWS,

OR THE DUMB "COMMENTS" THREAD,

ALL OF THAT STUFF

WILL GET STUCK IN YOUR HEAD

WE'VE GOT MORE SHOWS TO DO,

YOU CAN'T READ THE REVIEWS,

IF THEM HATERS COULD WRITE,

HOW COME THEY WORK FOR THE NEWS?

Oh, we're the Wee, Wee Navy

Freaking you out. That's what we do.

Freak freak the scene, here comes the Wee, Wee Navy,

in perfect harmony,

we're a bunch of freaks,

Coming at you by sea.

Wee, Wee Navy, on a freaky night cruise,

Wee, Wee Navy—seriously don't read the reviews.

(Dance break where the Wee Folk seem to be "exploring the space around them" and doing improvised pantomime, wide eyes filled with wonder.)

This was our introduction to the sea-based theatrical troupe known as the Leprechaun Royal Navy. The L.R.N. is the only branch of the military in Tir na Nog, other than the very corrupt weegee police.

The sailors, male and female, were unarmed. Or perhaps it would be more fitting to say they were armed only with skin-tight leotards and their atrocious singing voices.

The Leprechaun Navy was not nailing this number.

It was an abomination. I didn't even know where to begin. For starters, don't do a song with lyrics about being in "perfect harmony" when you are not remotely so. This is a no-brainer, but there's a strong argument to be made that the wee folk's brains are not fully developed, as they start drinking hard spirits and rosé wines when they are a mere one hundred years old.

Lily, who can hear a feather fall from a seagull 50 meters away, tried to bury her precious ears in the sand, howling in misery.

A particularly little wee woman with a tie-dye leotard and braids from her head to her shoes seemed to be in a completely different production.

If someone had choreographed this bit, there was no evidence of it. It felt improvised—*too* improvised. How, when these wee folk had been alive for thousands of years, HAD THEY NOT GOTTEN AT LEAST A LITTLE BIT BETTER AT SINGING AND DANCING AND EXPLORING THE SPACE AROUND THEM?

And to add a bit of insult to injury, if you don't like the leprechaun physique, you will certainly not like it stuffed into a leotard. It would be some time before I could un-see these wee little sausage-like people gyrating in my nightmares.

By the time Lily and I could process all of this amateur

theatricality, we had already been put in chains and hauled away on their longboat.

Under my glasses, I rubbed my lackluster eyes, surprised to see that we were suddenly aboard their little galleon.

That's the moment I learned that the true secret weapon of the Leprechaun Royal Navy is the "Wow Factor." While you're thinking, *Wow, this is the worst thing I've ever seen or heard*, you don't notice the little hands throwing you into shackles and whisking you away.

The Wee Navy doesn't carry weapons because they don't need them—they *are* the weapon.

Below deck, in her cramped-even-for-a-leprechaun-sized quarters, we were interrogated by Aileen Whose Luscious Eyes Sparkle Like Ten Thousand Emeralds in the Sun. Her cabin made up the stern of the ship, with a stained-glass window depicting the tacky leprechaun constellations. One wall contained the most lavish steam harp I have ever seen.

(A steam harp is the leprechaun version of a pipe organ. The leprechaun version uses steam power to annoy a set of sixty-six tiny, bird-like faeries called Plunkettes. A Plunkette looks like a hummingbird with a double beak like a tuning fork.

When the steam harp is played, a blast of steam annoys the Plunkettes until they fly out of a tube and pluck at the harp strings at the top of the instrument. It's rare to find steam harps, even in Tir na Nog, as Plunkettes are also delicious, with a taste that the wee folk liken to a human-realm mozzarella stick.)

Aileen was the ranking officer of the ship, a position called Troupe Captain Fabuloso. She wiped her tiny face off with a towel and chugged some whiskey from a squirt bottle. She was winded from the short dance number, but from the crinkles on her little walnut face, she seemed to be about three thousand years old (middle age for a leprechaun).

Hers was the unique leotard I had noticed from shore, done in tie-dye. Her white braids were connected all the way to her toes, where they were entwined to the laces of her jazz shoes with pointless bows.

Aileen was kind of pulling this off. For a leprechaun, which are among the ugliest things in any dimension, Aileen was not the worst of 'em. Not by a mile.

"Detective [gasp] Boyle, allow me to introduce myself. [gasp] Aileen Whose Eyes Sparkle Like Ten Thousand Emeralds in the Sun, at your service. I have been sent from His Serene Highness, Raghnall, to collect you [gasp] and the demon dog," wheezed Aileen.

Aileen with the oh-so-ordinary eyes stretched her legs, which were almost seven inches long, combined.

"But first, [gasp, pant] Detective Boyle, how did you like the number, because it's really a work in progress and I hope you can tell some of the choreography is just a place-holder until we can really work on it?"

"Ugh," I blurted out by accident.

Lily nudged me with her snout, to remind me that honest feedback is never what the wee folk are looking for, and especially not wee actor types.

"I meant . . . marvelous. We really saw the effort that went into it! You could tell that everyone was really trying."

"Oh, grand! It is shaping up pretty well," said Aileen, her face exploding with pride, fully believing in some false narrative that I had now just reinforced.

I was a tad confused about the business of King Raghnall "sending" for me and Lily. Between us, I didn't like it one bit. If the king had orders to collect me, I had zero doubt that it was not a favor, but for some icky reason.

"Your king has . . . *sent* for me?" I said, nervously rubbing my wrists against the iron shackles that chained me to Lily, then to the steam harp that dominated the tiny, sweat-scented room that Aileen was disgustingly filling with whiskey burps. "I do have business with His Serene Highness—the delivery of some of his leprechaun police force, who ran afoul of the laws of the Human Republic."

"Ooooh, ye have some weegees!?"

"Indeed, here in my vastsack with an injured old god called Crom Cruach."

With a sinister glint, Aileen's eyes shot like a laser beam to my Roscommon Football Club souvenir coin purse. By instinct, I reached for my shillelagh or my very nice umbrella, only to realize neither was at hand.

"How thoughtful of His Serene Highness to send us an escort," I said. "But I wasn't expecting to be escorted . . . by force? If that's what is happening here, Madame Troupe Captain Fabuloso?"

"Nobody's used a lick of force on ye yet, beefie!" chuckled Aileen. "That was a friendly dance number that we used with you. I don't think you or the devil dog would like to hear one of our . . . scarier numbers, in the key of F SHARP MINOR!"

With that, Aileen smooshed her tiny fingers into a terrifying chord on the keys of the steam harp. Lily and I jumped, bonking heads on the ceiling. One Plunkette flew too close to Lily's mouth and got eaten. Not Lily's fault; they smell so delicious.

Two female sailors with the shape and personality of eggs rolled over and took the vastsack while they poked at us with sabers. Aileen took the sack from them and locked it into a tiny green safe emblazoned with gilded Greek masks of Comedy and Tragedy.

"We'll hold on to those weegees for you for the moment, in the ship's safe, to which only I know the combination. You are our esteemed guest . . . for the moment, Mr. Ronan Beefie. Behave nicely and we'll keep it that way," chuckled Aileen, with breath that smelled like a distillery that had burned to the ground because of child labor law violations. "No funny stuff from you and the [takes a human minute to catch her breath] demon dog, and we'll be good as gold."

The female sailors locked the safe, spinning a dial that caused the Greek masks to change expressions with a mechanical groan. (Comedy became Tragedy and vice versa.)

Aileen's eyes danced, pleased as punch. She smooshed

her stubby fingers into the steam harp and performed a vocal warmup that would make Cerberus, the three-headed hound of hell, cover his ears with his paws.

I took offense to Lily, my best friend, being referred to as a demon dog. But she is huge, and depending on your size, you might think of her as a monster, too.

I considered the notion of fighting our way off of the ship and making a swim for land (yes, wolfhounds can swim, as all mammals can swim). But I also knew that we were badly outnumbered by these little freaks of the sea, and there was no way I could swim with Aileen's safe. Our best move would be to play nice. For now.

I forced a sly smile at Aileen, to give the impression that I was keeping a secret—which I was not. I wanted to make it *seem* like I had plan.

"We dress for dinner aboard the *Synging Millington*," wheezed Aileen. "Be on deck in half a spell, sharp. Black or white tie for the gents."

Then she fell backward off of the stool and needed me to help her up, like a turtle whose hair was braided to her shoes.

I saluted the little Troupe Captain Fabuloso and her face lit up. This was a breech of Special Unit protocol, as it is not encouraged to recognize the ranks of wee folk, which are sooooo arbitrary.

As I adjusted my uniform, Lily licked my face, the delicious trace of Plunkette on her breath.

Chapter Five
SPLEEN SOUP

I had no other clothing besides the uniform I was wearing, so I arrived at dinner on deck in exactly what I had on for the past week and a half, sporting shousting holes in the shoulder and various other signs of wear and tear.

Fortunately for me, a military uniform can be worn to a black- or white-tie event—this is covered in the handbook that comes with the Special Unit uniform and costs 25 euros.

The watermelon-scented seawater had done a real number on the main deck of the *Synging Millington*. With each step, one had the sensation of pulling one's foot off of a brand-new mouse glue trap. Poor Lily's pads, still tender from the shrapnel of E.R.B.s, were not taking the stickiness well at all.

The Wee Navy, about two dozen sailors in total, gathered at a long banquet table on the main deck. The tallest female came to my knee height. They were dressed in white tie and tails on the gents, lavish gowns and gloves on the ladies, with sabers and harps strung to their hips. Both ladies and fellows wore ridiculous plume hats and medals on every available millimeter of fabric of their chests. On a close inspection of one such medal, I could read the word *tinreamh*, which is the faerie word for *attendance*.

Aileen arrived last in a full suit of leprechaun armor made of solid gold. It was magnificent, thousands of years old, with filigree of a type that I had only ever seen back in Wise Young Jim's class. Unfortunately, this beautiful armor allowed her zero range of movement, so a half-dozen sailors would move her from place to place and put food in her mouth with a long spoon (also gold).

Lily and I were shackled in chains to one end of the table, which made us feel suspiciously like hostages.

Aileen wheezed inside the suit of armor, which probably fit her better at some time in the distant past. Her plump walnut face pressed out of the helmet, overflowing like a muffin top.

"Pureed spleen of toothless narwhal, Mr. Boyle, enjoy!" gasped Aileen as two tiny sailors set down steaming bowls of blubbery goop before Lily and me.

"Yum," I said with a level of sarcasm that could be registered from 400 kilometers above Earth at the International Space Station, "and silly us, Lily, we had pureed whale spleen for lunch."

Lily chuckled in the language of the animals, then devoured her bowl with appalling enthusiasm. Seems that blended-up spleen of a sea unicorn is the perfect taste for a wolfhound palate.

To be hospitable, I dabbed my lips with a tiny drop of the goo, using the wee wooden spoon that accompanied the bowl. I then quietly barfed over my shoulder. I would let Lily finish the rest of mine, and it seemed like she could have gulped down a dozen more bowls of spleen soup without batting an eyelash.

The dinner began with three hours of toasts. Leprechauns love to hear themselves talk. Each of the wee sailors was toasted by the others as being the all-time greatest something-or-other, and there was much keening and wailing, and everyone put their sticky shoes up on the table to show off how fancy they were.

The crying and hugging might remind you of full-sized Irish humans, who can be similarly inclined.

The dinner was a horrid fog of leprechaun burps and farts, somehow more disgusting than the soup itself. But the true horror was the game of charades that followed. If you've never seen a bunch of wee actors playing charades, nothing will make you want to pluck out your eyeballs faster. Oh, the milking of the bits, the mugging of the little wrinkled faces! Also, they were using themselves as "celebrities," which is a violation of charades rules in any realm.

Charades disagreements led to a brief but ultra-violent brawl amongst the wee actors, who at this point had all had far too much punch, and were no longer making sense. As much as they had sung about "freaking us out," they now were legitimately freaking me out.

Troupe Captain Aileen was dizzy and blurry. Four Admirals Supreme Numero Uno (lowest rank in their navy) hoisted her up and lowered her below deck on a little crane that seemed to be designed just for this purpose. Two surly maidens with ridiculous plume hats with sabers poked Lily and me below deck, where we were moved into a surprisingly comfortable bin of potatoes in the storage hold.

Stacked about the hold of the ship were a stunning quantity of leotards, wigs, fake noses, and random doorframes and staircases—all the bits you would need to put on an amateurish production of some terrible musical.

My wrist and Lily's leg were chained to a bilge pipe above our heads. Lily dozed off atop me, the unholy aroma of spleen soup searing a path across my eyes with each of her snores.

When the sweet seawater began to fill the room, I thought I was having a nightmare.

If only.

Chapter Six
MERROW ATTACK!

As I awoke, shrieking, the hold of the *Synging Millington* was a meter deep with seawater that was rising fast.

Lily chomped on the bilge pump above us, ripping it off the ceiling. This allowed my wrist and her leg to slip free. The ship rocked from side to side as we swam across the flooding cabin. I lifted Lily onto the crane designed for Aileen in her armor and cranked her up toward the main deck. Lily's density and the sticky gears took all of my strength. When Lily was safely on deck, she yanked me up like a puppy, by the shillelagh strap on my back.

The scene on the deck was, in a word: bananas. The Wee Navy, still dazed from rum punch, were attempting to mount one of their "Musical Attack Numbers" against a full pod of bloodthirsty merrows. Merrows are the sea-based faerie folk, whose bottom halves are iridescent fish and whose faces look like they've had too much plastic surgery. Their eyes and noses are pinched tight, as if someone standing behind them is pulling on their ponytail. Their razor-sharp teeth are in rows, like a shark's.

Three plump merrows were flopping about the deck. (Without legs, merrows are disadvantaged out of water.) They swatted at the Wee Navy with tridents made of coral.

To the port and starboard sides, another half-dozen merrows were biting their fangs into the wooden hull of the ship, trying to capsize the vessel.

I had never known that merrows *eat* leprechauns until the precise moment when I saw one of the wee sailors lose his footing and slide across the deck, directly into the fangs of a cross-eyed bullmerrow.

The cross-eyed bullmerrow looked directly at me as he

licked his chops. His nose was pierced with a brass ring, and his human chest tattooed with a heart labeled MUM.

The Wee Navy was one sailor down. A mist of leprechaun blood sprayed from the fangs of the bullmerrow. The good news: Leprechaun blood tastes slightly better than narwhal spleen soup.

The bullmerrow picked some leprechaun out of his teeth with the tip of his trident, doing a quick flossing.

Aileen was still in her solid gold armor, out cold. Four wee sailors were using her as a battering ram, knocking the merrows back underwater like Whack-a-Weasel.

The merrows responded with a ferocity that reminded me of my friend Gary, the Scottish Werewolf. I mean it as a compliment when I say: Merrows fight like Scots. Merrows lose lots of teeth as they fight, and in fact, they can sometimes do a weaponized burp, where they send their teeth flying like little missiles.

Here's a sketch of a single merrow tooth, so imagine a mouth with rows of hundreds of these.

Merrows cannot survive out of the water for more than a few spells, so I was feeling confident that we would survive this assault. After all, I had the world's most loyal 180-pound wolfhound at my side. In my biggest voice, I managed to shriek:

"GOOD AFTERNOON, MERROWFOLK! RONAN JANET BOYLE OF THE SPECIAL UNIT OF TIR NA NOG. THE WOLFHOUND AND I ARE ON OFFICIAL BUSINESS, CARRYING A VALID BEEFCARD. ANY EFFORT TO INTERFERE WITH OUR WORK, OR COMPLAINTS ABOUT US, MUST BE LOGGED— IN WRITING—WITH THE DIRECTOR OF THE SPECIAL UNIT, TIR NA NOG, KILLARNEY, HUMAN REALM, AND CC'D TO HIS SERENE HIGHNESS, RAGHNALL, KING OF THE LEPRECHAUNS, OIFIGTOWN, TIR NA NOG."

While this usually annoys most of the faerie folk (they hate to put things in writing) the merrowfolk just blinked their black eyes with a collective vibe of meh.

Just then, I felt a razor-sharp trident poke through

my kilt and into my behind, as the cross-eyed bullmerrow hoisted me like a pale teenage hors d'oeuvre.

This was the second time in a week that a mythical figure of Irish folklore had stabbed me, and I was, frankly, over it.

I was about to be munched upon by this bullmerrow who loves his mum and makes casual decisions about nose jewelry. I had the sense that, unlike my trip through Laura the Cavewhale, this would be a permanent stomach position that I would be filling.

Until the strangest turn of events unfolded before my sticky face.

The smallest merrowcow put out her (human-ish) hand and held back the arm of the bullmerrow as he was about to take a bite out of my face. The bullmerrow averted his eyes when the little merrowcow addressed him, in a manner of respect, which is when I noticed that the littlest merrowcow's head was formed into the shape of a small crown, as if the very bones of her noggin had been shaped into a royal hat as she grew (which I would find is exactly what happens to a princess of the merrowfolk when a new queen is hatched every five thousand years).

In my periphery, the Wee Navy sang a number called "Get Sweet, Retreat (Move Your Freaky Thingy into the Escape Dinghies)." And so they did, pulling the never-awakened-in-the-entire-fracas Troupe Captain Fabuloso with them, and rowing and/or mime-rowing away from the rapidly sinking *Synging Millington* in a set of cheerfully painted dinghies.

As if under a spell cast by the littlest merrowcow, the bullmerrow lowered me on his trident and took a strange, transparent blowfish from a pouch under his arm. He ducked his head underwater, then popped back up and exhaled into the fish, inflating its body like a balloon that was slightly larger than my head. The fish was yanked over my head, and then it puckered its mouth around my neck, creating a makeshift, yet airtight, diver's helmet.

The mum-loving bullmerrow pulled out another of these curious fish and made a helmet for Lily—who was not at all pleased with this occurrence, and tried her best to NOT be put into the blowfish. If you have ever put a dog into a Christmas sweater, you might imagine how putting Lily's head *into a fish* unfolded.

The fish on our heads are called the humanfish. Humanfish are a rare (but not mythical) sea creature that happens to thrive on carbon dioxide—the very thing us humans blow out when we exhale. Then the humanfish gets indigestion from too much CO_2, and their little spleen farts out O_2, the very thing that we mostly breathe up on land.

So Lily and I were alive, *albeit very freaked out,* while the *Synging Millington* capsized into the sea and the dinghies of the Wee Navy disappeared over the horizon.

The trident poke in my bum stung in the sweet seawater, which gave me something to focus on instead of the fact that Lily and I had fish on our heads and were being pulled underwater by bloodthirsty merrows.

In a bit of good news, I could no longer hear the Wee Navy's retreat song.

Chapter Seven
MERROWLAND

*L*iterally is the most misused word of the early twenty-first century.

If you say *literally* to Dolores, my hilarious pink-haired legal guardian back in Galway, she will give you a nurple twister, wherein she quickly twists the front of your upper pectoral muscle. And ouch, it hurts so so bad. I have learned to avoid the use of that word whenever possible. Smarty-pantses and Harvard-editing-book-Grinches will tell you not to use this word. So while I want to tell you that the below-sea Queendom of Merrowland is *literally* an underwater amusement park, I will instead tell you that it is *precisely* an underwater amusement park.

Keep in mind that I was wearing broken prescription glasses and looking out from inside the guts of a (somewhat) translucent fish burping just enough oxygen to keep me alive—here's an approximate scribble of the Queendom of Merrowland.

The bullmerrow and a half dozen other merrowfolk swam us up to the main gate, towing us along with their tridents. At the gate, our heights were checked and we were issued Day-Glo wristbands, which we were told were "good for rides, but NOT for concessions or snacks, or for the Coral Coaster, or the queen's 4D LiveSperience."

The bullmerrow gave a tiny smile as he saw my reaction to their Queendom.

"Welcome to Merrowland, beefie and hound. Yes, I know, I know."

"Your Queendom is so . . . amusing?" I said from inside my fish.

The bullmerrow chuckled, sending bubbles from the gills on his neck as he pulled us along.

"Aye, this is the Second Queendom, established on the ruins of the first one. Built in your year of 1940," he said, his neck bubbling. "The First Queendom before this was crushed by the sinking of a beefie ship called the SS *Athenia*."

"That would be the beginning of our second World War," I added, racking my brain to find the vague bit of human history that drifts around way in the back behind the *Lord of the Rings* trivia.

The bullmerrow's crossed eyes intersected further, not seeming to comprehend my trivial human-wars fact. He pointed his trident, and sure enough, a few hundred meters to my left, there was the rusted, barnacle-encrusted wreckage of an old human passenger ship. The name, *Athenia, Glasgow*, was still legible on the stern.

I gasped, which caused me to briefly inhale the human-fish's intestines into my own nose and mouth. The *Athenia* lay on the ruins of what looked like Atlantis itself—ivory pillars, now snapped and jumbled like Pick-Up Sticks. The remnants of an entire Greek city—amphitheater, forum—were all flattened beneath the rusting human ship. A merrow sculpture, which at one point must have been as tall as the Colossus at Rhodes, poked through the hull of the *Athenia*, making it look as if this merrow's trident had been the thing that sunk the ship.

"Yes, yes. I know, I know. The First Queendom was so much nicer," said the bullmerrow, sighing in a way that only a creature with gills can. "'Twas called Atlantis in our language, the greatest Queendom ever known, until it was flattened by your ugly human metal thingy."

"Ship," I said inside my fish.

"Sure, sure. *Ship*. Atlantis was our Queendom for five thousand beefie years, then—splat. In the chaos after the splatting of the first Queendom, Queen Feebee lived in exile, to the far west of the Atlantic. Off the shore of a bee-fie metropolis called Brook Lynn."

"Brook Lynn? Brooklyn, yes!" I said inside my fish helmet. Around this point, I realized that I should keep my responses brief, as the humanfish farts a very small amount of O2 and I was starting to feel woozy.

"While in exile, Queen Feebee would float on the surface and study the beefie metropolis at night. On her fortieth night in exile, she had a vision: She would return to Atlantis and build a Second Queendom—an exact replica of the glistening city of Brook Lynn that she had beheld across the sea."

I looked around as we floated through the main avenue of this garish merrow city, and while I can't say I was too familiar with the New York borough of Brooklyn, this did not look like what I had seen in any Spike Lee Joint. It looked more like—well—precisely like a seaside amusement park. Perhaps there is one of those in Brooklyn, but I had not heard of it. I made a note to ask Dolores about this back in Galway.

"It's . . . um . . . very nice," I lied convincingly, looking to Lily to back me up as we drifted past massive conch shells that served as concession stands. One sold something called "QUEEN FEEBEE'S FAMOUS FOOT-LONGS." Yet these foot-longs were diminutive, not the length of a foot in imperial measurement. That's when, on a closer look, I realized: These were hot dog buns filled with actual leprechaun feet. Along with seaweed, hot kelp, and a squirt of black squid ink. Yecch.

"Skip the foot-longs," said the bullmerrow. "They're deboned for tourists. Leprechaun feet without the bones in them are gross. The bones are what gives them flavor."

Lily looked at me, a curious look in her eyes as if to say WHAAAA?

"Yes," said the bullmerrow, "the disgustingness gives leprechaun feet 'umami' as it's called in the Sea of Japan," apparently reading Lily's mind, which is not something either Lily or I knew he could do.

"Sorry, I should have warned you," the bullmerrow explained. "We use telepathy in the Second Queendom for convenience, as talking with a mouth underwater while having neck gills is a kerfuffle," thought the bullmerrow directly into our minds with a pleasing little tickle of electricity. "If you don't mind, I'll just think at you now, as it saves me a bit of air and a lot of logistical hassle."

"Of course," Lily and I thought to him politely.

We floated past a coral booth where a pufferfish with too much eye shadow was blowing on a pipe, clearly thinking about the great disappointments of her life. A sign above her head advertised: I CAN GUESS YOUR WEIGHT IN ANY REALM. Beside her, in another stall, a narwhal feigned a smile at us while quietly wishing for his own death.

"One ring on my horn and take home a stuffy! Three tries for ten euros!" said the narwhal, pleading with us to end it all for him with his eyes.

The bullmerrow hustled us along, and his brain sent us a little zap of embarrassment.

"The Second Queendom is, well . . . it's kind of tacky, I know," thought the bullmerrow. "Really, the first Queendom was way nicer. So nice. Come, Her Highness has invited you to tea, which means you must be of some importance."

Tea with Her Highness meant being strapped into a spinning teacup ride with Queen Feebee (the littlest merrowcow with the head that had grown into a crown).

My wristband was checked by a pink octopus with a patch over one eye, as was Lily's, which was affixed to her foreleg. We took our seats in the teacup car and more than ever in my life did I wish that I did not have even a tiny bit of Whale Spleen Soup in my stomach, as I was certainly about to quietly barf out whatever remained.

Queen Feebee swam in and was belted in by her lower fish-half by the bullmerrow, who bowed to her, and then signaled with his mind that Lily and I should do the same, which we did, tilting our fish-sealed heads in respect.

Queen Feebee's Madcap Teacup Mayhem (the full name of the ride) is a swirling nightmare in the category of carnival ride that I would call "Hard to Enjoy." Lily and I both closed our eyes as the teacup we sat in began to spiral like mad on the arms of a mechanical octopus-shaped contraption.

In my peripheral vision, I noticed a tiny look of envy that the sad, eye-patched, real octopus who ran the ride gave to the mechanical octopus who was the ride. I cannot imagine what their relationship was like from day to day.

As we spun around like laundry that was about to bake,

Queen Feebee sent us a welcome song directly into our brains. The song went something like this:

> *Welcome to the Second Queendom,*
>
> *Get a wristband, be our guest.*
>
> *Welcome to the Second Queendom.*
>
> *Sorry it's not as nice as the First.*
>
> *But that one got crushed,*
>
> *by a big human thing,*
>
> *So I made up this one,*
>
> *which looks just like Brook Lynn.*

To be polite, Lily and I both thought a version of "Oh, it is so lovely here, thanks for having us."

Soon I realized that while I could hear the thoughts of Queen Feebee in my mind, I was *also hearing Lily's thoughts,* crystal clear.

"Yes, our merrowfolk telepathy is so strong that you are picking up the thoughts of your friend the big red hound as well," thought Queen Feebee directly into the language part of my brain.

"Wow. Your head is like some kind of Wi-Fi station. Neat!" I thought back.

"I know not what a *Wi–Fi station* is," thought Feebee. "But I am told that my crown makes my telepathy extra-strong. Now then, what business have you with our enemies and favorite footlong ingredient: the leprechauns? To aid or abet the Leprechaun Navy is an offense punishable by one thousand years in our Koo Koo House."

With her mind, she send us a postcard of the Merrowland "Koo Koo House." The entrance was a spinning tube, which led to wacky stairs, and a sort of funhouse. On first mind-glance, this Koo Koo House seemed pretty amusing.

"Trust me. The Koo Koo House is *not* fun after a thousand human years. Explain yourself, beefie, or be sent there without delay, and without wristbands, which means you will have to buy a new ticket each ride, for one thousand years, which in human euros will be over one billion euros."

"Oh, Your Highness!" Lily thought, loud enough for me to hear as well. "The human beefie and I had been captured by the Wee Navy while on official business. He has a valid Beefcard, and we are en route to Oifigtown to deliver some wee prisoners."

"Oifigtown?" thought Feebee loudly. "To see Rahgnall, King of the Leprechauns? He's literally the ugliest thing that has ever lived in any realm. Think to me more about these wee prisoners and why I should not make them into delicious foot-longs post haste."

In about a minute, I thought to Queen Feebee the entire history of events that led me to this moment—the changeling in the oubliette at Connemara, training at Collins House, my parents being framed by Lord Desmond Dooley, the brought-back-to-life Bog Man . . . and yadda yadda yadda.

"ENOUGH. I get it," thought the little queen, a tad bit snippy. "And where are these weegee prisoners of yours right now?"

"I'm afraid they're at the bottom of the sea, locked in a green safe in the *Synging Millington*," I thought to the queen, "a green safe with the masks of Comedy and Tragedy on it."

"Aye. The Wee Navy loves theatrical bric-a-brac. Their love of musical theater makes eating them even more satisfying for my people. I have no doubt that the Wee Navy had planned to release your prisoners and leave you and the hound adrift at sea. That's just what those wee devils would do, and they'd sing an underrehearsed song at you while they did it. Awful little things. If the Wee Navy could make five euros by selling their grandmother to a zoo, they would do it. If you don't believe me, go visit their Wee Grand-mother Zoo off of the Aran Islands."

Sharing Queen Feebee's brain Wi-Fi, Lily and I both pictured an actual "Grandmother Zoo" and wondered what they would even charge for this sort of thing. Of course, in Lily's mind, the grandmothers were wolfhounds.

Side note: If you ever get the chance to inhabit someone else's head, do it—it's a real eye opener! You'll be pleasantly surprised to find: OTHER FOLKS ARE NOT THINK-ING ABOUT *YOU* ALL THE TIME. They're not replaying all of your mistakes and faux pas and awkward high fives and judging you on an endless loop of shame. I did a quick search of Lily's brain to look for thoughts about me and was surprised to find only: "Ronan Smells Friend" and "Ronan Beret: Handsome." And that was it. Everything else was Lily's thoughts, about Lily's life! Whew, what a relief!

"Well, you are in luck, beefie. I, Queen Feebee, First of

her Name with All of the Wristbands, shall see that you and your prisoners are delivered to Oifigtown without further hassle."

Lily and I shared an excited look from our fish-headed-heads. I bowed, probably too many times.

"Thank you, Your Highness," I thought to her. "Honestly, it's been a rubbish week and I would love to wrap up my mission and find my parents, who have escaped a human prison and whose whereabouts are currently unknown. Also I am probably in need of medical attention from a human doctor."

"Again, I don't need your whole sob story," thought Feebee. "Do not thank me. It is part of my royal vow to help a Special Unit Officer in need. You and the hound will be safely in Oifigtown by eleven A.M. tomorrow."

"Oh yes, because of my Beefcard?"

"Ha. No. A valid Beefcard is more useless than a pink wristband is for the Koo Koo House. But your beefie leader, Special Unit Commissioner McManus, is well-known to me."

"You know the commissioner?!" I thought excitedly. (The commissioner is a silver-haired man with a kind face, and the one who personally promoted me to the rank of detective.)

"I know him well. Very well, in fact. Before he was in the Special Unit, your Commissioner McManus was a young fisherman from the port of Cork."

"And you . . . met him?! How neat."

"Met? Ha. No. It's a bit more complicated than that. The beefie word would be *marrried*. Your human commissioner is my ex-husband."

"Oh." I thought, dumbfounded by this detail, and not having any sense what a person should say to a queen of a mythical race that used to be married to your human boss back in Killarney.

"It was a weird time for both of us," thought Feebee. "He was nineteen, I was three thousand. I was singing on a rock one day, trying to lure fishermen to their deaths, which is my thing—all young merrowcows do it, it's a phase—and young Colm McManus crashed into my rock.

We got to talking. We were both into music, and he was certainly handsome, for a bipedal creature. And well . . . I wish I could say it ended well, but it did not."

"Oh. Oh?" I stammered in my brain, starting to feel like this was Too Much Information.

"I guess part of me was thinking: Feebee, your parents want you to fill your role and become Queen of the Merrowfolk, but you've just met this handsome beefie fisherman, and maybe you two could get a place off Dingle and make some records, maybe do something practical on the side, to make the ends meet—a little bakery or something. Maybe a bakery that has a little performance space in the back, for intimate shows. Make a little money, but mostly make it about giving back to the community. Maybe do some poetry slams, have nights where we taste wine and do paintings. Make our own matcha teas and such. But for sure, make it a safe space for artists, to workshop things, without judgment. Maybe we get a kiln and do a pottery class on Wednesday nights . . ."

As Queen Feebee was thinking her *entire backstory* with Commissioner McManus to me, my mind started to wander. When I snapped back to reality, I realized we were still spinning in Queen Feebee's Madcap Teacup Mayhem. I barfed—ever so briefly—at which point Queen Feebee's face turned into a vicious scowl (merrows can look absolutely terrifying with just a slight adjustment of their singular eyebrow).

"I can hear you're bored by my backstory. 'Twas a complicated relationship made more complicated by the fact that I can't survive on land for more than a few spells. But I still have a lot of love in my tail for Colm McManus, and as a courtesy, I shall personally deliver you to King Raghnall in Oifigtown."

"Bless you, Your Highness," I thought.

"And then, when you have concluded your business with King Raghnall, I shall fulfill a promise that I made a long time ago," thought the queen with a devious smile that showed her rows of shark-like fangs.

"And what was that?" I asked in all of our minds.

"Oh, simple," giggled the psychic energy of the queen. "To eat him."

And with that, the little octopus with one working eyeball brought the ride to a stop, and we were unloaded, dizzy, queasy, and now accessories in a murder-not-yet-transpired.

"Assemble the Royal Phalanx!" blasted out the queen to the minds of everything within ten nautical miles. "We'll retrieve the prisoners of this brave Special Unit Beefie and make for Oifigtown."

A collective gasp of thoughts and bubbles erupted from the merrowfolk around us, bonking into our brains so hard that Lily and I both winced in pain.

"Yes, brothers and sisters! TOMORROW WE DINE ON RAGHNALL, KING OF THE WEE FOLK!"

The merrows shook their tridents in celebration in a way that looked like slow motion, as we were underwater. Lily looked at me and sent the thought, clear as a bell: "It just can't ever get easier, can it, Ronan?"

"Apparently not," I thought, as our wristbands were sliced off by the bullmerrow's trident and two dozen of the strongest merrows you've ever or never seen lined up in rows, brandishing tridents and pikes of jagged coral and shields made from the half-shells of some type of giant oyster. This was the queen's "Phalanx," which is really a fancy name for a bunch of merrows making a wall around you.

Lily and I were in the central spot, with the cross-eyed bullmerrow and the little queen herself, and soon we were moving across the ocean floor at a good clip.

Our swim back to the wreckage of the *Synging Millington* was uneventful, at least from inside the phalanx, where most of what we could see were the butts of armed, riled-up merrowfolk.

The bullmerrow—whose name turned out to be Durant—had us describe Aileen's safe in the captain's quarters in our minds, and then he transmitted our description into the brains of two sleek merrowcows who swam into the wreckage to retrieve it.

At this point in my new relationship with the merrows

and Queen Feebee, the novelty of sending one's thoughts to those around you had worn off completely. If you ever spend time with merrows, and I hope you do, you will soon learn that you are spending ninety-nine percent of your energy trying *not* to think inappropriate things, as they are immediately put *on blast* to the brains of those nearby. In a short span of time, I had accidentally thought things like this:

Was Durant born with crossed eyes, or did they "stick like that" after making a funny face as a child?

Queen Feebee talks WAY too much. UGH, WHEN WILL SHE STOP TALKING?

Merrow butts are weird-looking. They can't actually poop from these, can they? WHERE DO MERROWS POOP FROM???

I really wouldn't want to live amongst the Merrows in this tacky Second Queendom and thank goodness all I can smell is the inside of this fish and not sizzling leprechaun feet on buns.

Did Durant get that "Mum" tattoo from a licensed tattoo artist? Because it looks homemade. I think he did it himself.

And, of course, the merrows hear all of this in their minds *clear as a bell*. What gets interesting is how they politely stop responding to your thoughts—a trick they must have spent centuries perfecting. Still, you can see in their faces a tiny but significant bit of tragedy every time you think something.

I tried my best to think nothing about my immediate surroundings or the strange fish butts of the merrowfolk. Instead, I thought hard about my parents, escaped from Mountjoy Prison and missing somewhere in the Human Republic of Ireland. I worried at the top of my thoughts about Log MacDougal, my best friend, dangerous psychopath, and loving sidekick who had chased off after Lord Desmond Dooley back at the River of GLOOM. And then, on top of all of these worries, I harkened back to Pierre the Far Darrig, still pinned to a wall high in the Steeps, and how I had vowed to return for him one day (time and weather permitting).

The sleek merrowcows returned with Captain Aileen's safe and presented it in slow motion to Durant. (Everything merrows do *looks* like it's in slow motion, per the being underwater bit.)

As the phalanx swam, two giant oarfish soon appeared, pulling in ahead of and behind the phalanx, respectively. In my mind, Queen Feebee answered my silent question about the oarfish, explaining that a Queen's Phalanx is always escorted by oarfish, because even though they are not mythological creatures, they are so creepy-looking that almost anything in the ocean swims away from them. These two oarfish (both of whom were named Meghan by sheer coincidence) were 17 *meters* in length. If you haven't seen a giant oarfish lately—check one out. I'll wait here in my ongoing narrative.

See?

The Meghans were so long that I could almost never see all of them. I could make out the head or the tail of either, but never both of both.

I had now been deep below the surface of the ocean for over a spell. While I was getting some oxygen from the humanfish, the pressure of the ocean depths was starting to make my head feel clamped. I tried to remember some simple details about myself, as a test. I know that my middle name starts with the letter J . . . Right? *Ronan J. Something?*

As we swam, I tried not to telegraph my nervousness to Queen Feebee. So I kept my eyes on the safe, in Durant's arms. Inside of it was my Roscommon Football Club vast-sack, with all of my weegee prisoners, the undead Bog Man, and not to mention my very nice umbrella. Were they even still alive in there? Or had they perished like fireflies kept in a jar? Would my nice umbrella even work again after I had used it to stab the Bog Man through the heart?

And my biggest worry: How would I prevent my new friend, Queen Feebee, from eating the King of the Lepre-chauns and did she just hear me think all of these worries?

Since I couldn't stop these thoughts, I made an effort to think of a song very loud in my head, as a smoke screen. And if you know me, you'll know when I worry, I visit a fic-tional version of Dame Judi Dench in my mind. Currently

Dame Judi was singing Taylor Swift's "Bad Blood" while doing a little hip shake with it. This tactic must have been working, for when I caught Queen Feebee's glance, she was happily bopping her crown to the tune playing in *my* head.

It wasn't too long before my feet started to touch the sandy bottom of the seafloor, while my fish-encased head started to poke out above the surface. We had walked up and into the wintery port city of Oifigtown, seat of the Leprechaun Royal Family.

It was a snowy November morning at 11 A.M. when we surfaced, as it's *always* that in Oifigtown (the same as it's always 8 P.M. on a Friday in Nogbottom). The royal palace loomed above us, with spires and towers poking into the sky in amusing shapes and colors. Despite the snow flurries, we were about to receive a surprisingly warm welcome from King Raghnall.

Chapter Eight
LI'L FLOTILLA

As we surfaced, my humanfish burped itself off of my head with a pop that would make my ears ring for weeks.

Lily shook off her fur in that fun way that dogs do, and as we scanned around, she and I sent each other a loud mind-thought: "*Holy farts.*"

For awaiting us in the icy harbor was a (not-figurative) flotilla.

That I remembered the word *flotilla* was a surprise even to me, as I was definitely feeling brain damaged. This time underwater had cost me at least a few IQ points. *Where was I? What was I supposed to be doing? Who is this big friendly dog? I'm sure all of these details would come back to me at some point??? Am I using the right number of question marks????*

The ships of the flotilla looked like—and in fact, were—regular wooden clogs. The kind you will see for sale at the gift shop at Schiphol Airport, Amsterdam, The Netherlands.

King Raghnall's flotilla is fifty pairs of women's size 7.5 wooden clogs, each with one with a leprechaun inside, using it as a kayak, steering with a little paddle of solid gold.

The flotilla was delightful to watch, as the snow and intermittent sunbeams dappled off of their paddles and glowing cherry noses. It seems the main goal of this flotilla that had come to greet us was to try not to fall out of their clogs into the harbor.

The Queen's Phalanx was now half out of the water, surrounded by this amusing flotilla. Both Meghans departed in graceful slithers along with the humanfish.

Three-score ships were docked all around us in the harbor, some leprechaun-sized, but others in different scales, giving me the impression that this busy port serves many types of faerie folk. I spotted a fishing trawler with a crew of far darrigs, a fully rigged Japanese wasen, staffed by something that looked like the ghosts of cats with oversized eyeballs, and a Scandinavian cruise ship for gnomes, which must bill themselves as "clothing optional." The entire ship was a floating gnome discotheque. At the stern, I could make out a little foam bar, where the gnomes who were *not even wearing underwear* were truly, sincerely grooving.

I made a note to store that image somewhere far away in my mind and hopefully not see it again until the very moment of my own death or perhaps not even then.

I glanced over to Durant, the green safe still in his grip. I checked in on Queen Feebee, and with a little smile she sent me the thought: "I get it, Ronan, you're in love with this Captain de Valera person."

HA! I was certainly not thinking about Captain de Valera, nor about how I had accidentally told her I loved her AS A GOOF back in North Ifreann.

"NO! Not at all!? THAT'S SO DUMB," I thought as hard as I could.

"Ugh. Give it a rest," bounced back Queen Feebee. "This beefie with the good haircut and the two-color eyes is, like, ninety percent what you think about. You pretty much never stop. Don't stress. It's normal to have these feelings. How do you think I almost opened up a poetry-bakery with your handsome two-legged friend Colm McManus? Stop beating yourself up about every little thing. Now play it cool, beefie. And don't forget: If you blow my plan to eat King Raghnall, then I'll eat you and the hound instead. These teeth aren't just for show."

This was distressing. Not just the threat of being eaten, but the fact that Captain de Valera dominates my subconscious mind in ways I am unaware of.

I shook it all off as best I could and, poaching some of the brain-Wi-Fi off of Queen Feebee, I sent a thought over to Lily: "Let's just play nice for as long as we can, dump the weegees, and get the heck out of here."

And Lily thought back: "And how, Ronan? My paws are killing me."

The Li'l Flotilla (their official title) started to row their clogs around us, doing some synchronized kayaking. They slapped the surface of the water with their golden paddles as they made a syncopated a capella song of coughs, grunts, and farts that really made a big impression.

A wee woman with bright blue hair whose body was the shape of an eggplant paddled her clog up to Queen Feebee, giving a half-bow, which felt a tad sarcastic, as if the wee woman didn't really recognize the royal status of Feebee (which of course Raghnall's court does not).

The blue-haired woman maneuvered awkwardly over to Lily and me, bobbing like a cork on the water—looking very much like she had never been on the water before this moment.

"Name, rank, Beefcard, if you please," said the blue-haired leprechaun curtly to me while giving Lily serious side-eye.

"Cheers," I replied, tipping my beret, which was soaked and would probably never regain its ideal shape. "Ronan Janet Boyle, Detective Special Unit of Tir na Nog with official business to see your King Raghnall." I presented my damp Beefcard, the passport that allows humans to travel in Tir na Nog.

The blue-haired woman took my Beefcard and efficiently blew her nose on it, then mimed wiping her bottom with it as well (a classic sort of leprechaun "bit" that was hilarious to her and her mates). Then she handed the card back to me.

"And the hellhound? Official business as well?"

"Aye, madame," I replied, "Lily, Detective Wolfhound Special Unit, we carry the same rank."

The wee woman paddled clumsily back to the Li'l Flotilla and consulted with her wee mates. After some hubbub, the blue-haired woman pulled out a tin whistle and played a lively tune on it. In the blink of an eye, an enormous red crow appeared in the air overhead, circling above us.

"Alert the Royal Kitchen!" the wee woman called out to the red crow. "A welcome banquet must be prepared for the Beefie, Officer the Hound, and Her Serene Highness, Queen Feebee, First of Her Name with All of the Wristbands."

The crow nodded its beak and was about to fly away when then blue-haired woman added, with a passionate bit of snideness, "And have the kitchen set a KIDDIE TABLE FOR OUR MERROWFOLK FRIENDS!"

OOF. Wow. So much shade thrown at the marrows. This would not end well.

The crow flapped off into the snowy sky, disappearing into the comical spires of the city above.

"The Beefie and Hound shall ride with the King's Guard to the high palace. Merrowfolk, sorry for the inconvenience, but per your annoying insistence on being in water *all of the time*, you'll have to use the sewer entrance to the palace, just to the left of this harbor. Follow the smell of poop and you'll know you're in the right place! We'll see you when you get there—follow the signs that say SERVICE ENTRANCE and try not to touch anything."

Queen Feebee smiled her razor-sharp teeth with a legitimately evil smile. It's not some casual preference of the merrowfolk to stay in water, it's the only thing that keeps them alive, and it was clear the blue-haired woman was going out of her way to make things horrible for them.

"Be safe, Ronan Beefie," thought Queen Feebee to me, "and we'll see you at the high palace. And not one thought about my plan to eat the king, do we understand each other?"

I nodded to Queen Feebee as she and the merrowfolk

flapped their tails and swam toward the mouth of a hideous open sewer that emptied out into the harbor.

Lily and I slogged up onto shore, where I accidentally caught my last glimpse of the clothing-optional gnome cruise ship, and holy cow were those gnomes having the time of their lives. The thumping of the gnome-techno music would ring in my ears for the entire journey up the snowy streets of Oifigtown to the high palace.

Chapter Nine
THE POTATO KING FOR DINNER

The capital of Oifigtown is actually an island connected to the mainland of Tir na Nog by 301 bridges, although the leprechauns themselves will tell you that many of those bridges are imaginary, so check with the locals first before you try to walk on them.

The architectural style of the town is one that the wee folk call TurntupTurnip—which means the tops of the building look a bit like the domes of Russia's Kremlin, either in comical onion, turnip, or mushroom shapes. Some of the buttresses of the palace looked like they were made from hard candy.

Leprechauns get more powerful the smaller that they are, and since Oifigtown has been a seat of faerie royals for many thousands of years, the wee folk who live there have evolved to be really super-tiny. The average building of Oifigtown, including the Royal Shoe Mint, comes just below Lily's haunches. The residents, who stared slack-jawed at us, clocked in around 14 to 18 inches tall.

At the embankment of the harbor, the flotilla transferred us over to King Raghnall's Mounted Guard, which is a dozen leprechauns small enough to ride on regular Yorkshire terriers—the official "steed" of the royal line of leprechauns dating all the way back to the human year of 1861 when Yorkies were invented in England someplace.

Make no mistake: The King's Mounted Guard is cute. Like, really, off-the-charts, they-should-have-a-TikTok-account cute. But if you're expecting some level of Austrian Lipizzaner horse precision out of them, forget it—*that is not part of a Yorkie's raison d'etre.* Our procession up the fancy little boulevards of the capital was frequently sidelined by the Yorkies sniffing, peeing, checking where they had just peed, then digging for unseen rats that must have existed below the streets (likely in the sewers that the poor merrows had been relegated to).

Without a sense of time, the wee folk didn't mind that our journey through town took an entire spell of seventy-two minutes. A journey that, if Lily and I had been walking *without* a fleet of Yorkies, would have taken about thirty seconds.

The high palace stands three wolfhounds high, with glistening turnips of pure gold and platinum atop the spires, and flying buttresses painted in candy-cane stripes.

Lily and I were led over the drawbridge and to the main banquet hall, which was lavishly decorated with battle flags and tiny suits of armor. Atop the long tables were bouquets of shamrocks.

In a seated position, Lily and I could both just fit at our tiny table without bumping our heads on the crowded gallery above.

Lily and a gray female Yorkie consulted briefly in the language of the animals, and soon Lily was brought a blanket, bowl of water, and steaming pot of some kind of stinky stew that dogs must like. Lily snarfed it down in the blink of an eye, then cozied herself into a furry croissant at my ankles and drifted off to sleep. I couldn't blame her, as ever since we left Capitaine Hili on the *ucky evil*, neither of us had slept for more than a few moments, at best. Between that and the lack of air under the ocean, I was pretty worm-tied about the snape of my brane. State. State of my BRAME. BREEEN. YOU KNOW WHAT I MEAN, THE THINK IM-SIDE MEE HAT? HEAT? HEART-HAT. Okay, between us, part of me was VERY concerned that my time with the merrows had given me PERTI-NENT BREIANE FROMAGE. Wait, is that what it is even crawled?

A balcony of several hundred well-connected leprechauns milled about just above my pathetic beret. Down below, a throne made of (real) unicorn horns stood at the head of the room on an elevated dais, at which a wee group of delegates sat. I cannot say for sure what each of the representatives was, but among them I noted: A Japanese y rei, who was the ghost of a toad, wearing a lot of Kabuki makeup. A Scottish Cat Sith—which was easy to spot as it was talking cat wearing a Glasgow Rovers football jersey, sipping on an Irn-Bru. The Cat Sith was whispering something to a Hawaiian menehune at her side who looked like a buff version of a leprechaun with glorious trapezius muscles, a grass skirt, and a lei of flowers that would bloom/die/rebloom every few seconds.

The blue-haired woman entered, now in a ladies' saffron kilt and shoes that looked like the disco balls in some Lady Gaga version of an awards show for pianos.

"Detective Boyle, welcome to the seat of King Raghnall, Most Beloved, Most Hilarious, Solid All-Around Mate and Friend to the Birds," she said, pulling up a chair that was clearly supposed to be human-sized but could barely contain my narrow bottom without a major squeeze.

"A few ground rules for when His Highness enters, as I'm guessing you've never met any member of the leprechaun royal family?"

"No, ma'am," I said.

"First off, don't scream. He looks a bit like a potato with eyeballs."

"It would never occur to me."

"Splendid, but if you do shriek or laugh, just act like you were shrieking or laughing about some funny or horrifying thing from your past, and he'll forget all about it."

"Check."

"Other than that, be yourself, do not pick him up, and have a nice time. That's really all. Oh, and . . . since we will be joined by those awful merrowfolk tonight, a portion of the hall will be flooded for their convenience, so watch where you step."

"O'course."

"Also, the merrowfolk act nice, but there's quite a bit of nasty history between them and His Highness, so if it gets snippy, just hang back and remember it's not your fight. Sound good? And I said 'be yourself,' yes?"

"Yes. Brilliant!" I said out loud, and then I very clearly thought about Queen Feebee's plan to eat King Raghnall. I waited for a response from the blue-haired woman, but as telepathy is a trait of only the merrowfolk, my message was not sent, but just stuck in my now certainly damaged brain, inside a soggy beret that I had once really loved.

"Anything else you're worried about?" prodded the blue-haired woman, just letting it hang there forever.

"Nope. Not really. Well, perhaps one little detail I should warn you about . . ."

I just had to say something. I was about to blurt out Queen Feebee's murder/dinner plan, but just then we were interrupted by the tooting of a conch shell, and a little hatch was opened at the lowest end of the room, flooding everything up to the dais.

Durant swam in, followed by the members of the phalanx, and at last, Queen Feebee herself. Durant still held on to the green safe with my precious cargo inside. The phalanx looked precisely like they had just spent some time in a leprechaun sewer and were none too pleased about it. The fact that they were allowed to openly carry their tridents and pikes into the banquet hall, considering their bad blood with the leprechauns, was surprising to say the least.

The delegates on the dais stood up (or floated in the case of the ghost toad) as the merrowfolk swam in.

Aren't we lucky, here they come.

Welcome, you fish-folks, to Oifigtown,

proclaimed the blue-haired woman, adding a sarcastic raspberry with her mouth.

The leprechauns in the gallery above gave a sad bit of golf applause. There was clearly not much love lost between these two mythical societies.

Queen Feebee nodded at me, sending the message, "Hi. If you told them my plan: YOU GET EATEN."

And the thought I sent back, shamefully and truthfully, was "I didn't say a word!"

The blue-haired woman crossed the dais and whacked a harp with a riding crop. The harp woke up and began to play a ferocious, blazing bit of hype music.

"AND NOW . . ." bellowed the blue-haired woman, "LET'S MAKE SOME NOISE FOR THE MAN HIMSELF. TWENTY-SEVEN CENTIMETERS OF PURE LUCK. THE THUNDER FROM THE UNDERNOG. THE BLAR-NEY STONE FELL IN LOVE WITH *HIM* WHEN HE

KISSED IT. THE UNDISPUTED KING OF THE LEPRE-
CHAUNS: RAGHNALL WITH THE SIZZLING BEACH
BODY!"

Except for the merrows, the place went berserk. Some
way too dangerous for the indoors fireworks were set off, sending flaming rainbows of fire through the room, bursting
into shapes of the leprechaun constellations, which I could
only tell as a CYCLOPS EYEBALL-BUTT shape exploded
millimeters from my nose.

Lily leaped to her feet and howled, as all dogs do at
the unexpected arrival of fireworks. On the dais, the buff
menehune started doing cartwheels while juggling flaming
torches. The Japanese toad ghost split into three versions
of itself and soared about the room, like a ghostly version
of the Blue Angels stunt planes. For no reason I'll ever
understand, the Scottish Cat Sith
started doing push-ups with a
deadly seriousness, bottle of
Irn-Bru balanced on her back. A
far darrig selling King Rahgnall

programs, souvenirs, and noisemakers approached Lily and me, but as I was out of euros, I declined, sending the far darrig muttering something unprintable about beefies as he went.

When the tiny king himself entered, the letdown from all of this hype was stunning.

A little man shaped like a potato with arms and legs waddled out onto the dais. His face looked painted on, as if the artist had *never seen a face before*. His eyes were looking in three different directions despite the fact that there were only two of them. His nose was that of a pig, *verbatim*, no changes. He had a large yellow tooth that jutted up from his little mouth.

"Cheers!" said the wee king as he waddled, doing a version of the dance that humans would call the "Cabbage Patch" before he plopped into the throne of unicorn horns. "Nice to see you all! Relax and be yourselves! I'm your king, but I'm also JUST A GUY!"

Huge cheers for this last bit, and the wee folk in the balcony bowed and curtsied with all of their might.

The blue-haired woman leaned in to the tiny king and whispered something in his ear. King Raghnall gave a wink to me, and then one to Queen Feebee.

"I'm told we have some distinguished guests?" chimed the wee king. "Randy Boyle from the Special Unit, and Her Serene Highness Feebee of the Second Queendom. YOU'RE VERY WELCOME, PLEASE BE YOURSELVES, I AM JUST A GUY!"

Queen Feebee rose up on her tail, coming half out of the flooded part of the banquet hall, doing a trick I had once seen a dolphin do for a fish at some egregious sea park that has now been cancelled.

"King Raghnall with the Sizzling Beach Body, foreign representatives of the faerie folk, I thank thee for the welcome. Per our accord with my ex-husband of the Special Unit, I have delivered the beefie detective to you, along with this safe from the hold of the *Synging Millington*."

A gasp went around the room. The sinking of the *Synging Millington* was already known around Oifigtown.

"A great tragedy," said the blue-haired woman. "The

greatest and fastest of His Majesty's ships, the crew still unaccounted for. I'm certain that despite our political differences, the merrowfolk did whatever they could to help the brave sailors of the *Synging Millington*."

Queen Feebee wiped a fake tear from her face while chuckling in her mind like a goblin. (It seems that leprechauns cannot pick up the telepathy of the merrows, perhaps from clouding their own minds with thousands of years of whiskey.)

"We bring three gifts for Your Highness," said Durant. "Wristbands of pink, green, bright pink, and gold!" One of the sleek merrowcows swam toward the dais, presenting a pike with dozens of wristbands—the type required for rides in the Second Queendom, and completely worthless anywhere else.

"Okay, neat," said Raghnall the king who displayed no qualities of a sizzling beach body, and was, it seemed, more like a potato that had been brought to life by a genie with limited powers.

"The gold wristband is good for my 4D LiveSperience

as well," boasted Queen Feebee, as if everyone knew what this meant when in fact none of us did. "And for concessions, but not the guess-your-weight booth."

"Super," yawned Raghnall, while letting out a not-that-quiet fart.

"The wristbands may not be transferred or exchanged, and please consult with any of the octopi on staff for black-out dates, of which there are many."

"Oi, I get it. What's the second gift?" said Raghnall, looking to move this along.

"The beefie himself, and the safe from the hold of the *Synging Millington*."

Durant swam up to the foot of the dais and set down the Comedy/Tragedy safe with some royal flourish.

"Blah blah blah, and that's two gifts with no cash value," said King Raghnall out loud, which seemed pretty aggressive. "I find your gifts tedious, you can skip the last one."

"But the last one is the very best!" said Queen Feebee. "It's something I promised a long time ago. But I have to whisper it into your beautiful wee ear. *Right. Into. Your. Ear.*"

Queen Feebee couldn't help but reveal her razor fangs as this last very frightening bit slithered out of her mouth.

Raghnall made a "whatever" gesture, and the blue-haired woman motioned for Queen Feebee to approach the dais. I wrapped my arm around Lily, who had fallen back asleep, and tried to think of a plan to prevent Queen Feebee from eating the little king, that I could enact within the next few seconds. *So far nothing on that.*

The king waddled up to the lip of the dais, bending over. Queen Feebee paddled up to him on her tail, licking her rows of fangs.

"Closer . . . closer . . ." said Queen Feebee in a stage whisper as the king leaned his ear within millimeters of her deadly maw.

"WAIT!" I screeched out. "KING RAGHNALL! I NEED TO TELL YOU SOMETHING! SOMETHING PRETTY SPECIFIC AND RIGHT NOW!"

"O'course," said Raghnall, "right after Her Highness tells me this secret present of hers, I'll get to you, beefie. Now make with the secret, fish breath."

And then, with a snap of her mouth, the little king vanished into Queen Feebee's face.

Feebee slurped, burped, then picked her teeth with the tip of her trident, a satisfied smile on her face. King Raghnall was gone, in one disgusting gulp. It happened so fast that many folks in the room didn't understand what had happened until Queen Feebee dropped her trident like a rap-battle microphone and said, "How ya like me now, you walking turnips?"

A panicked melee ensued as the wee folk above and below on the dais screamed, tumbled over themselves, tore out their hair, and wept and keened. Some tried to leap into the suits of armor, to mount some sort of counterattack, but it was not to be.

The merrowfolk retreated with a sublime level of organization. With a few shakes of their tails they disappeared back into hatch that led back to the sewers.

As they disappeared, Queen Feebee gave me a wink, then made a rude gesture that involved making a terrific toot sound with her human hand in her armpit, then blowing it like a kiss at the wee folk.

"The merrowfolk keep their promises," said Queen Feebee.

Durant grabbed the pike of wristbands from the dais and took it back. The merrows were gone. As efficiently as a Navy SEAL team of creatures that looked remarkably like actual seals.

Lily and I were dumbfounded. We had just been witnesses (and even accomplices) to a REGICIDE?! Yikes!

And then the wee folk and guests on the dais did something quite bizarre. Everyone picked up their little chairs, dusted them with a napkin, and politely returned to their seats.

The blue-haired woman held up her nubby little fingers, counted down from ten, and then the entire King Raghnall's entrance happened *again*.

"And now, smack your mitts and the place where you sits! Weighing in at three POUNDS four OUNCES. The Wee Man with the plan. He's suffered the slings and arrows AND HE TAKES NO MALARKEY FROM THE MERROWS—THE ACTUAL KING RAGHNALL!"

And in a replay of events, a tiny man, part twig, part

living piece of beef jerky, bounded onto the dais as spry as he could, considering his shoes were platinum lifts encrusted with a billion euros worth of precious gems.

A wee assistant rolled a harp onto the dais, and Raghnall played a brief solo upon it with his nose. A far darrig brushed Raghnall's floor-length beard. From a sprinkler system in the ceiling the crowd was misted with what smelled like Powers Whiskey.

Raghnall high-fived the delegates on the dais and plopped into his throne with a giddy fit of laughter.

Brothers and sisters, a welcome to you,
And apologies for this elaborate ruse,
But every few spells (it's no longer a hunch),
Queen Feebee tries to eat Raghnall for lunch,
The first time she did it—
I barely survived,

So I made up a plan so our kingdom could thrive.

And now her faux-murders all land with a thud,

For I send in my double: Dan, The Enchanted Spud.

Yes 'twas a potato the queen just imbibed,

(stuffed, just for fun—a unicorn turd inside).

This charade succeeds, you may not expect,

for the merrow's unrivaled knack to forget.

For at least nineteen times she's made me a dish,

And then they just forget, with brains like goldfish.

Say a quick prayer for Dan, 'twas a lovely potato,

(I painted his eyes on myself, so you know).

And welcome to Oifigtown, we're delighted you're here,

And don't shed a tear, when Feebee "eats" me next year.

And with that, the Royal Clog and Harp Orchestra paraded into the room, playing King Raghnall's Theme Song, the lyrics of which are in the old leprechaun language, and I could not understand. Everyone laughed heartily, as apparently this same "Feebee eats the king" bit happens annually. I cannot tell you how relieved I was. Not only was I not an accomplice in a regicide, it also meant far less paperwork when I got back to Collins House.

Dinner was served, which in Oifigtown style was nine courses of "Crazy Bread." A few of the breads had a recognizable counterpart in the human realm (soda bread with chocolate chips, for example) but some were truly crazy, in a medical sense. Apple Fritter-N-Critter was a deep-fried bread where the taste of apples was overwhelmed by some kind of mythological critter with a sharp little beak and talons. Luckily, the unicorn Crazy Bread was just shaped like a unicorn, with no actual unicorn meat or parts.

Midway through the dessert course, Lily and I were approached by the blue-haired woman, who escorted us to the dais to the tiny king himself.

"Remember, do not pick him up," said the wee woman. "I know it looks like it would be fun."

"Ronald Yvette Boiled!" called out the wee king, butchering my name with a good-natured chuckle.

I had been told that the wee king was "the ugliest thing that ever lived, in any realm," and while that was *technically true*, it should also be noted that the king's tiny face (while a bit of an architectural jumble) exuded a rare type of joy that is contagious. Within a spell of sitting with the tiny king, you'll find your cheeks hurt from smiling. Perhaps it's an actual magical spell, perhaps it's joie de vivre, but even Lily's mouth was curled up in that version of a smile that wolfhounds can do.

"You found the place all right? Sorry about the merrows, all of the faerie folk of the sea are a bit of a chore, if you ask me. That's why my navy has specific orders to attack those devils on sight, with six- or even eight-part harmony."

"Thank you, Your Highness. Our journey to Oifigtown has been, well—more eventful than I would have hoped for. And sorry about your Wee Navy."

"Oh, they'll turn up. They always do!" said Raghnall with a wink. "I sent them to collect you, but I hear there was a slight detour."

And just then, the doors of the hall burst open, and the Wee Navy "frolicked" in, their tiny hips gyrating, in a half-cocked musical number called "BACK IN BIZ-U-NESS."

Yes, "biz-u-ness." Not a word in English, Irish, or the language of the animals. I cannot explain. This tune was louder and slightly catchier than I was expecting. Poor Lily with her super-hearing buried her head in my armpit to muffle the sound. The last few wee naval officers freak-danced their way into the hall carrying Troupe Captain Aileen (still in her golden suit of armor and still very much asleep). Had she never awakened since the sinking of the *Synging Millington*? It's entirely possible.

"Now then, Detective, I'm told ye have some of my officers of the Wee Gaiscíoch in your possession?" said the king, using the official name of the weegees.

"Aye, Your Highness, in my vastsack, now in that green safe. Per the 1979 accord, I have delivered them to you, as they have committed crimes in the Human Republic of Ireland."

A team of wee folk slid the safe toward us, and a little man lit a clay pipe, puffing hard until the embers glowed bright blue. Then he used the pipe like a welding torch and melted the Comedy and Tragedy faces right off of the safe. The door landed with a heavy *thunk*, and the blue-haired woman pulled out my Roscommon Football Club vastsack.

It occurred to me that Aileen could have easily opened the safe with the combination, but perhaps nobody wanted to wake her up? Or perhaps leprechauns just prefer the hardest, least logical way of doing things.

"It's a vastsack, careful please!" I called out. "Besides your wee police officers, there's an ancient mummy and a nice umbrella inside." (Leprechauns invented vastsacks to steal large, human-sized things—so I didn't really need to remind the wee folk how to handle it.)

"Janice will draw up a receipt for the weegees, o'course," said King Raghnall, making a "draw up a receipt" gesture to the blue-haired woman whose name was now known to be Janice and somehow fit her so perfectly that I should have guessed it.

Janice handed the vastsack to me, a smile on her face, but a hand on her shillelagh, as if to say "don't get any smart ideas, beefie."

I reached into the sack and, with a bit of fumbling and a bit of the wee folk biting my fingers, I extracted the weegees and placed them before the king as gingerly as I could. Lily picked up the wee woman whose nose looked like it was put on upside down, just to keep her at bay.

"I MIGHT HAVE KNOWN! RED SHEILA OF THE BOUNCY HAIR AND THE TURNIP KREWE!" shrieked King Raghnall.

"Your Highness with the Sizzling Beach Body!" replied the little red-eyed woman who had been a thorn in my side for as long as I could remember, as she flailed, dangling from Lily's mouth.

"This beefie says ye have violated the laws of the human realm, is that so?"

"NAY!" shrieked the red-eyed woman as her little gang cursed, kicked, and spit, looking for ways to escape from the banquet hall.

"IF YE BE LYIN', SHEILA, IT'S A THOUSAND SPELLS IN THE BUTTER MINES FER YE!" howled King Raghnall, with literal smoke billowing from his ears.

"Fine," spat the little red-eyed woman as she let out a precise fart to show how annoyed she was. "We may have bent a few laws of the beefie realm. We'll get out of your luxurious hair. But let us keep the bog mummy! The one called Crom Cruach!"

"NAY, YA DAFT NITWIT!" fumed King Raghnall. "THAT BEEFIE LORD DESMOND DOOLEY HAS WARPED YER TINY BRAIN, SHEILA! HE'S GOT YE BOWING AND SCRAPING TO CROM CRUACH WHEN YER ONLY TRUE KING IS MESELF, RAGHNALL WITH THE SIZZLING BEACH BODY."

Raghnall did a little flex of his biceps that was perceptible only to him.

The king gestured to Lily that she could set down the wee woman. The red-eyed woman shuffled and fiddled, snorting out some vague version of "Sure, sure."

King Raghnall was displeased. He gave a little nod and from the shadows of the hall, a few surly Yorkshire terriers padded in, blocking any escape routes for the weegees. The Yorkies growled in a way that humans would find cute, but the wee folk find distressing. Lily and what looked like the captain of the Yorkies exchanged a bit in the language of the animals.

"Donut Boggle," said the king as he leaned into me, bungling my name in a way that made not even me recognize it. "Sheila has been a wart on my bum for three thousand years. She's a bad apple, her and her little krewe of Crom Cruach. But do not let a few stinkers ruin your impression of the wee folk!"

With a resounding "hear, hear," the wee folk of the gallery chimed in.

"Sheila and her wee devils were incited by that sinister beefie Lord Desmond Dooley. If I could get my hands on that pointy nose of his, I'd snap it in two."

"Lord Desmond Dooley is known to you?" I asked.

"Dooley! Of course. That beefie scoundrel? I know him all too well. You know he's not an actual lord the way I am king. It's his actual first name!"

"I know, right? Who does that?"

"Your friend Dooley has been pilfering Tir na Nog for our leprechaun treasures for a many spells. He's stolen entire henges belonging to my ancestors. He swiped the nose ring of the Brown Bull of Cooley! I've had reports that *my own favorite pipe* is for sale in his gallery," said Raghnall. "Like it's some sort of memorabilia!"

"In his creepy gallery on Henrietta Street!" I shrieked along enthusiastically. "Indeed! Dooley deals in stolen treasures. Lord Desmond Dooley is my enemy. He got me into all of this mess!"

I explained to the wee king how the pointy Lord Dooley had stolen the bog mummy from my parents' flat in Galway. How Mum and Da had been sent off to Mountjoy Prison for the crime, and until I returned him to the National Museum in Dublin, my parents would be fugitives.

(I skipped a few bits: Living with Dolores, Ireland's most intense fiddle player. Training at Collins House with Yogi Hansra. Never getting to properly know my fellow cadet called Tim the Medium-Sized Bear. My feelings for Captain de Valera, who I am ninety-nine percent sure I am not in love with at all, despite the fact that she hovers over my mind like the sword of Damocles in vinyl boots and with a better haircut and pretty great jawline. And of course, the one brown, one green eye that makes it look like her eyes are keeping secrets even from each other.)

"Red Sheila, I hereby revoke your leprechaun name of

Red Sheila with the Bouncy Hair. From henceforth ye shall be known as Other Sheila from the Butter Mines," proclaimed the wee king with a wave of his minuscule hand at the red-eyed woman.

She howled and shrieked, pulling out her own hair.

"Ninety-nine thousand spells in the butter mines for ye and yer krewe. Take them away!!"

And with a level of violence that I did not expect from Yorkshire terriers, Sheila and her evil little crew were yanked out of my life forever.

"This calls for some nonsense!" said the wee king, as, with a bit of help, he removed one of his platinum shoes, licked his finger, and rubbed it around in a loop from the heel to the tongue. The opening of the shoe started to sing, making a gorgeous tone like Waterford crystal. The wee folk up in the gallery did the same, and this was the first time I ever witnessed a leprechaun *tonein*. To my knowledge, I may be the only human who has ever seen one of these, as it must be started by a living king of the leprechauns and there's only been three of those in all of history.

The wee folks' golden shoes rang out like Tibetan singing bowls, creating such a joyous harmony that the vibrations began to lift the wee folk into the air. Just a wee bit at first, a centimeter or two, and then, as the vibrations of the tones grew, and reverberated off of the walls, everything in the room started to float—myself and Lily included, turning the banquet hall into a humming anti-gravity chamber.

At first, I could feel the tonein song in the fillings in my teeth, then like a kaleidoscope of butterflies, the feeling migrated to my stomach. Lily must have been feeling it too, as she was doing that wolfhound version of a smile again, and then, suspended by the music, she rolled over onto her back, rubbing herself in the sound.

The wee folk let the tone die out, and we all drifted back down again, and King Raghnall let out a tiny burp as if to punctuate the song, reminding us all that leprechauns *cannot* just let something be nice. They have to "leprechaun it up" a bit.

"Logan Turtle," said the wee king, destroying any

semblance of my name. "What would ye say if I offered ye a wee bribe to bring me back this Lord Desmond Dooley? He must stand trial in here in Oifigtown. And when I say wee bribe, I'm talking about my guest closet, which is taller than you, filled with shoes just like these ones."

I snorted out a bit of the four-leaf-clover tea I was sipping as the king proposed this—an illegal and totally inappropriate violation of my oath as an officer of the Special Unit. Somewhere I even had a pamphlet that cost several euros describing *just how illegal it is to accept bribes from the wee folk*. As I'd noted: The bejeweled shoes the king was wearing now (while I am not a jeweler, or commodities broker) had a street value in the human realm of approximately, let's say, a billion euros.

Now he was talking about a guest closet full of shoes like these—with an unfathomable price tag. Just for doing something I was pretty much planning to do already.

"Oh, Your Highness!" I stammered. "I would be sent deep into the Joy Vaults for accepting a bribe of even a single euro. When I recited Recruit's Pledge at Collins House,

I also signed a contract that specifically forbids me from engaging in such activity."

"Are ye quite sure, Detective Go-Nuts-at-the-Shrimp-Broil?"

Now I was pretty sure the king was messing up my name just to toy with me, and it was keeping Lily very amused.

"Quite certain, Your Highness."

"Well, that's a tragedy. I've been meaning to clean out the guest closet of its golden and platinum shoes, which honestly make these ones look like harpy turds. But if ye cannot bring me Lord Desmond Dooley, I'll just have to take care of him meself," said the king as his googly-eyes drifted off to the middle distance.

I looked to Lily, who gave me a firm nod with her fuzzy rust-colored head. An idea began to form deep in my damp beret. I knew in my heart that even if I were lucky enough to capture Lord Desmond Dooley, he would never see real justice in the human realm. Dooley is well connected and corrupt to the tip of his so-called nose.

Perhaps what the wee king was asking was not only

possible—but could be the only way Dooley would ever be brought to any semblance of justice.

"But . . ." I muttered, leaning closer to the king's tiny, misshapen ear, "the capture of Lord Desmond Dooley is my sole remaining vendetta. While Dooley is well connected in the human realm, I could, if authorized by the Special Unit, deliver him here for trial before Your Highness."

"Brilliant!" giggled the tiny king as he tapped his little fingers together in a way that behaviorists would describe as diabolical. "And then when ye've delivered Dooley to me, I'll send him for a life sentence in the Butter Mines, and you'll get that guest closet of me old shoes."

"NO. ABSOLUTELY NOT," I replied, making it crystal clear that I was not going to be part of this bribe even though a tiny part of my brain was considering it.

"Sure, sure, that's what I said," said Raghnall, tapping the side of his red little nose. "Ye bring me this beefie devil OUT OF THE GOODNESS OF YER HEART, and I'll give you . . . *not* my closet of bejeweled shoes. Just a firm handshake and the satisfaction of a job well done."

Raghnall and the blue-haired woman both held in a laugh until their faces looked ready to pop. The notion to leprechauns of doing something "out of the goodness of your heart" is hilarious to them. Leprechauns are in it for gold, shoes, spells, and smells. There is a T-shirt of this exact slogan sold at buggy stops in Tir na Nog.

"So we won't shake on it. Since me giving you that pile of treasure ne'er seen by beefie eyes is something we are DEFINITELY NOT DOING," said Rahgnall, now holding on to the blue-haired woman so that they didn't fall over in giddy hysterics.

"Yes, Your Majesty. Absolutely not doing that," I said, not using any kind of irony or sarcasm because I was not entering into a "treasure for measure" agreement with King Raghnall, despite how much he kept insisting on it.

"Splendid! So it's agreed. Ye shall bring Dooley here, alive . . . or in some kind of covered dish, whichever is eas-ier. And I, Raghnall with the Sizzling Beach Body, will not provide you with a guest closet full of the rarest golden and platinum shoes, some with magical powers, and some that even look good with white slacks. Also, if you are only able to bring Dooley's head, that's also fine."

"Thank you, Your Highness."

"What will you need for this mission? I can provide you with up to three hundred Yorkshire terriers, and many fit volunteers from my Wee Navy."

I laughed so hard that tea shot out of my nose. The notion of returning to the human realm with hundreds of lapdogs and a C-minus musical theater troupe was just not something I was up for.

"Um. The wolfhound and I are good on our own. Just some guidance to a geata back into the human realm, Your Highness. Preferably one that lets out near the human town of Killarney?"

I remembered that the faerie folk have entirely different names for all of the counties and towns of the Human Republic.

"That is, sire, a passage toward the lake that holds the Monster of Lough Leane," trying to be specific about my destination in a way the wee folk would understand.

"AYE! MonsterPuddle!" laughed Raghnall. "The creature of MonsterPuddle!"

"Indeed! What you call *MonsterPuddle*, we call *Lough Leane*. Near the human town of Killarney. Is that lake monster known to you? Long neck, scaly? Looks a bit like a dinosaur?"

"MUDBUG?! Aye. Mudbug the lake monster is not a mythical creature. That jerk is an actual dinosaur, left over from the last ice age. And get this: Mudbug is *not* related to the Loch Ness Monster—but he tells everyone that he is! So annoying! He's really just a random leftover spinosaurus. Nessie is mythical, Mudbug is SO VERY NOT! *Poser.*"

Some wee folk on the dais nodded, while others dozed off, their stinky little feet slipping out of their solid gold shoes.

"But I know the spot whereof you speak and there's a geata right in the middle of the local Beefnog* less than a spell from MonsterPuddle and Mudbug the Rando."

---

* *Beefnog* is Faerie slang for any human town.

"A geata in the Beefnog of Killarney?" I exclaimed. "This would be ideal, Your Highness!"

"Cill Airne!" woofed Lily, saying Killarney's name in the language of the animals.

"We'll get you to your Beefnog, but please—you must take some of this food to go. We made way too much."

Next was an exchange that exists in both the faerie realm and the human realm, where the host insists that you take some leftovers with you, while you say, "No no, you're too kind, but we're stuffed." And they say, "But you could make a casserole!" And on and on. As I was nursing several weeks of injuries and carrying an undead pagan god in my vastsack, I really, truly did not want to take some leftover Crazy Bread back to the human realm.

But this was not the hill I was going to die on.

Half a spell later, Lily and I were loaded up with a half-dozen plastic containers of leftover Crazy Bread that I did not enjoy the first time around and had no plans of turning into a casserole. I placed all the containers in my vastsack and did a quick check to ensure that the Bog Man was still was still undead, or dead—most importantly, *not awake and making mischief.* The good news was the poke through the heart with my very nice umbrella had done the trick, and he had maintained the aspects of NOT BEING ALIVE that I had come to appreciate since North Ifreann. The bad news was my very nice umbrella had a fair amount of "undead bog mummy gunk" on it and would likely never work well again.

The blue-haired woman led us to one of the highest turnip-shaped spires of the palace, which is known as the Royal Transport Station. For security purposes, King Raghnall with the Sizzling Beach Body has an enchanted butter churn that can connect to any of the thousands of faerie gates in the Human Republic of Ireland. Of course, like everything in the palace, it was on a scale for wee folk, so Lily and I had to take the journey as "split singles."

With a smile, wink, and some fierce churning, I was zapped out of Tir na Nog and into a place that was vaguely familiar. A mirror, a sink, a small Mayan calendar . . . by the time Lily plopped on top of me, I realized that we were back in Killarney. Specifically, we were in the clean, well-lit men's restroom of Casita Mexicana, one of Ireland's top Mexican restaurants.

Chapter Ten
A LADYSHIP IS FORMED

After eating every vegetarian item on the Casita Mexicana menu, Lily and I raced back to Collins House. If you're ever in Killarney, try Casita Mexicana. And if you're ever a vegetarian, high five from me, Ronan Janet Boyle.

After not nailing the secret song that reveals Collins House, Lily and I burst through the doors, greeted by the smell of five hundred years of paperwork related to the crimes of the faerie folk.

I felt a strange lump in my throat. Collins House felt like . . . home. Not so long ago, I was an intern at the Galway (Human) Garda office, working for the indecipherable

Captain John Fearnley. And now, here I was, back from a journey across Tir na Nog. No longer just Ronan Boyle: *cadet who barely passed Tin Whistle for Beginners.* Now I was Ronan Janet Boyle: teenage bad boy, survivor of the swamp of certain death, and guy who is pretty much in control of his food allergies.

I stood up very straight, gave Lily a stroke on the head, and with panache, called out to the main hall.

"Oh, hello again. LOOK WHO'S BACK!"

And to make it even juicier, I pulled the vastsack from my sporran and gave it a sassy twirl. I held my heroic posture for an awkwardly long time, and—nobody noticed.

"UM . . . DETECTIVE BOYLE AND LILY THE WOLFHOUND! BACK FROM THE MISSION THAT COMMISSIONER MCMANUS SENT ME ON. THE VENDETTAS. VENDETTI. THE UNDEAD BOG MAN?! GOT HIM IN MY COIN PURSE! *NAILED IT! YOU'RE WELCOME!*"

I would love to tell you I DID NOT do a little moonwalk dance right here, to punctuate the moment, but that wouldn't be accurate.

Sergeant O'Brien, the púca who works the front desk, looked up, in her donkey form, a pen in her mouth, equine ears akimbo.

"For the love of God will you shut up, boy? I'm trying to write down people's lunch orders."

And then a jump-scare as Pat Finch appeared. His face looking like something Stephen King would concoct to pop out of abandoned wells in a fictional version of Maine.

"Did you say sumpin', lad?" grunted Pat Finch. "Are ye lost?"

"Pat Finch! It's me: Detective Ronan Boyle, back to see Commissioner McManus! A celebration is in order. And perhaps some medical attention. Lily and I are back from Tir na Nog with the bog man known as CROM CRUACH!"

"That sounds neat. Remind me who you are again?" said Finch.

"RONAN BOYLE!" I proclaimed in a way that sounded more like whining than I had intended it to. "Do you not remember me at all, Pat Finch?"

"Oh . . . sure. O'course. Wait . . . didn't you die on Frolic Day?"

"NO. That was Brian Bean from Kells. The one who does impressions—now a ghost."

"Wait, are you the Medium-Sized Bear?"

"OF COURSE NOT! That's Tim the Medium-Sized Bear."

"Well, you're sure not the handsome one with the eye patch."

"Dermot Lally," I groaned, annoyed. "No. I'm Ronan Boyle! The pale, unlikely cadet with the missing parents who's been on these remarkable adventures that I'm writing down in vivid detail."

"Oh, grand," said Pat Finch as if he'd never heard anything about me or my adventures. "Way to go, guy. And o'course I remember you. Skinny fella. With the big dog."

And then, Pat Finch leaned in, put his hand on my shoulder, and said, with gravitas, "Did you want to put in a lunch order? We're getting Casita Mexicana."

The lump of pride in my throat took a cliff dive to my stomach, where it became a Mexican-food-themed *tragedia*. Apparently my adventures were a bigger deal to me than to other folks at Collins House, who had their own fires to put out and had been going about their day-to-day lives as if I weren't pulling off remarkable acts of derring-do! It made me wonder why I was even keeping this detailed diary!

"We're good. In fact, we just had Casita Mexicana," I told Finch, pouting as visibly as I could.

"Oh, brilliant. And if ye've got evidence from your little field trip, that goes to processing, Domnhall."

Pat Finch confidently called me by the wrong name and departed without fanfare and without handing me some kind of medal, which, honestly, would not have been totally out of line.

Lily looked at me doing a small shrug with her eyes that is even more powerful than a human-shoulder type of shrug.

"Boyle!" called out a voice I associated with pain. I turned to see the tiny, stunning, and quite deadly Yogi Hansra, my shillelagh safety and combat officer. "You're back, boyo!"

"I am! In fact, I thought there'd be a tad more fanfare about that part?"

"Oh, Detective Boyle, one of the many downsides to

being one of Europe's most secretive law enforcement agencies is that every mission is *so secret* that we never get to celebrate anything. How was your trip? Very secretive? Secret accomplishments achieved, I hope?"

"Yes, pretty big ones."

"Splendid. See you in my hot yoga class at three P.M. It's ninety minutes, all flow, crow poses, inversions. No cowards."

And Yogi Hansra departed, doing a completely silent cartwheel through the lobby and parkour-ing her way over a family of far darrigs who were waiting at the bail desk.

Sergeant O'Brien called out. Now she was a crow, but with her same glasses on. "Boyle! Stop posing for a statue and get yer skinny behind up to the commissioner's office on the double!" she cawed as her pen skittered out of her talon.

Lily and I bounded across the main lobby and did something only a true Collins House noobster would do: We jumped into the Unreliable Elevator. *Whoops.*

The Collins House elevator is so ancient and dilapidated that it runs on an extended-warranty spell cast on it by an Underqueen of the Harpies. And just our luck: The Ghost of Brian Bean was hovering about inside.

"*Ronan Boyle was the case that they gave me*," rapped Brian Bean doing a better impression of Snoop Dogg than anyone has ever heard on the planet called Earth.

"BRIAN BEAN!" I beamed, and went for a hug, falling through his ghostly vapor as my face bonked against the elevator wall. "Thanks for everything, Brian. To say none of this mission could have happened without you would be an understatement!"

"Oh, please, Ronan. Happy to help. Bouncing between the land of the living and the realm of the dead, it's nice to find moments of normalcy, you know?"

"O'course."

"And GOOD NEWS!"

"Yes, very good news! You heard? I'm back with Crom Cruach!"

"Oh, brilliant. Fun. But I meant: *Good news for me*. I've finally perfected my Tom-Hanks-reacts-to-Lady-Gaga impression."

"OH. Oh?" I replied, a deathly pall falling over my face.

I should point out: Brian is *amazing at impressions*. Second to none. But boy-oh-boy can they get tedious.

"Want to hear it?" queried Brian as his phantom body hovered.

Long pause. My eyes darted to the elevator's display panel—somehow we were ONLY on the third floor, heading to eleven. CURSE THAT UNDERQUEEN OF THE HARPIES.

"I can't wait," came out of my mouth, to everyone's surprise, including my own.

Seventeen human minutes later, I had seen Brian transformed. The impression was perfection. Brian would do bits of famous Gaga numbers: "Poker Face," "Shallow," etc., and Tom Hanks would react, saying things like, "Whaaaa?! WAAAOOW!!! HOLY CAAAOW!"

I had no idea that Tom Hanks had such a distinct tone. And somehow when Brian did Gaga—he started to *look* like Lady Gaga. It was magnificent. The only little detail I *might* change, were I lucky enough to see it again, is that nobody needs seventeen minutes of that. And if I'm nitpicking, why was there a whole section where Forrest Gump sang "Paparazzi?" Amazing? Yes. But sooooo self-indulgent, and almost an entirely different bit.

When the elevator screamed to its near death at the eleventh floor, I "hugged" Brian again, because even while he cannot be touched, it felt like the right thing to do.

Lily and I bounded to Commissioner McManus's office, which is equal parts library and medieval crime lab, with a stunning view of Lough Leane. Peat logs were burning in a fireplace so big that an eighteen-hand unicorn could stand up inside of it.

Atop a mahogany desk was a dog bed; in it, what for all the world looked like a sleeping chimpanzee with wings. Did the commissioner have some sort of flying monkey—the likes of which have only been seen in movie musicals of yore? I decided: Don't mention the sleeping chimp with wings until someone else does.

Commissioner McManus was pointing his sad and handsome face out at Lough Leane. At his elbow was the forgettable Deputy Commissioner Finbar Dowd—a man so bland that if his face were ever to appear on a milk carton, he would be upstaged by the barcode.*

Now that I'd met the commissioner's first wife, Queen Feebee, I understood his stares off into the middle distance. How often is it that learning one detail about a person changes the way you understand them forever? Was some part of the commissioner always thinking about a little pottery and poetry shop near Dingle and the undying love of a middle-aged merrow queen?

In the shadows, quietly twirling a brand-new purple shillelagh in one hand—a copy of Yeats's *Collected Poems* in the other—was Captain Siobhán de Valera. I didn't even have to see her completely to feel her epic presence.

In the glow of the peat, I caught a glint in the captain's green eye (but not the brown one) as Lily and I entered. I doffed my beret and gave a little bow, which merited an actual laugh from the captain.

---

* *Finbar Dowd here, ME HAVING FORGETTABLE LOOKS IS UP FOR DEBATE. More than four people have said I have the "ideal face for amateur character acting," which is one of my many hobbies in Killarney, as well as being a CHEWING GUM VIGILANTE! Toss chewing gum on the sidewalk in Killarney, and you will meet FINBAR DOWD, SIDEWALK AVENGER!*

"Detective Boyle, Lily," said the captain, coming over and giving Lily a terrific scratch under the neck. "Welcome home."

Was I a tiny bit jealous that I didn't get a scratch under the neck? *Yes. Yes I was.* Not because I'm in love with the captain, NO WAY. That's dumb. She's just my regular old boss, who was back to her normal self after a bad harpy bite, and had just gotten a pretty wicked new asymmetrical hair cut and it really seemed like the captain's new haircut had a streak of purple in it, which was reflected in her nail color and the new shillelagh that she was spinning with silent proficiency. That purple theme was contrasted with a matte black lipstick that was perhaps a bit of camouflage, or just a solid choice for her face. Either way she was crushing it.

And then, because if you're like me, a very big thought can create a train wreck through your brain in a fraction of a second, taking out billions of innocent synapses. Was I *in love* with Captain de Valera or did I want to *be* Captain de Valera? Thank the old Irish gods that Queen Feebee wasn't around to hear all of this internal turmoil rattling in my fromage-d Brian.

Were my feelings for the captain romantic, or just hero-worship? And what really is the difference? If I am, in fact, in love with Captain de Valera, isn't that really just a desire to have her personality become permanently part of my own? Is my seemingly schoolboy crush just really a wish to achieve the confidence that the captain exudes? Or could both be true?

Then I wondered when she got the new shillelagh and how much had it cost in the Supply and Weapons Department, which overcharges for every little thing. Then I wondered how birds work, which made a strong case that *my Brian was not what it once was.*

"BOYLE! ARE YOU ALL RIGHT, SON?" thundered a voice, snapping me back to reality.

"Did you go away for a moment, Boyle?" asked vague little Finbar Dowd.

"Me?! No sir. Not at all, Deputy Commissioner. Right here at your service," I said.

"Oh. Because you gazed at Captain de Valera, then you got a faraway look, and then you mumbled, 'Do I want to be Captain de Valera?' *out loud*. Then it seemed like you missed the whole medal ceremony because you were lost in some sort of inner turmoil and then you asked us how birds work."

I looked down at my jacket, shredded from my recent travels, to see there was a *brand-new medal* on the breast pocket, with the Irish word *Luach* upon it.

"Oh, neat!" I blurted out, making a mental note to look up what *luach* means.

"So you *didn't* miss it? The getting the medal part? And the commissioner's toast and his kind words? Because it seemed like you had zoned out," said Dowd.

In my left hand I saw I was holding a glass of Diet Craic, a rare faerie drink that is made with fifteen percent changeling tears and gives you the very specific feeling of walking on new carpeting with bare feet.

"Right, o'course!" I bluffed, tossing back the Diet Craic, "I heard . . . that whole bit. And for sure, nobody needs to remind me how birds work. *All in the old Brian up here.*"

How long had I been zoned out? Did the Commissioner make a long speech while I gazed at the captain and thought of becoming her versus being in love with her? Was I muttering these thoughts out loud right now?

WORSE: WAS I ACTUALLY PERMANENTLY BRIAN-FROMAGED FROM MY RECENT ADVENTURES? THE CAVE WHALE STUFF, THE UNDERWATER STUFF? AND THAT'S NOT THE RIGHT WORD. BRAIN-FROMAGE? BRAIN'S-DRAINAGE SERVICE?

"Boyle, come back, lad!" said the commissioner's voice, which happens to sound like Yo-Yo Ma playing the hits of Ennio Morricone.

The commissioner stepped over to me, placing a hand on each shoulder, which sent a zap of pain from the poke hole I had acquired back in the Shousting Dome.

"Lad, I think I speak for all of us when I say, yes—we are concerned that you have a bit of brain damage," said the commissioner. "The phrase you cannot remember is *brain damage*—not *Brian's fromage,* which would mean *Brian's cheese* in French. We'll have the Mysterious Doctor Boiko check you out right away. He did wonders on Captain de Valera after her harpy bite."

"Indeed," said the captain, clicking her shillelagh into the brass hooks across the back of her new pleather morning coat, "I'm fit as a fiddle again."

"Captain de Valera," I said, wincing with my injured shoulder as I gave a salute, trying to be super-casual. "Hopefully not too many details of our battle with the wee folk in North Ifreann have been scorched into your memory."

"It's a bit of a blur, Detective Boyle," said the captain, with a sly smile on her black-lipstick-coated lips that made me sweaty and dizzy, and seemed to imply that she did recall some of my embarrassing fanboy-dom.

The commissioner cleared his throat. "I understand you have the bog man known as Crom Cruach in your possession?"

"Indeed, Commissioner," I replied as I pulled the

Roscommon Football Club vastsack from my sporran and placed it in his hands, which are somehow also kind of handsome. "If he had drunk the captain's blood in that wicked ceremony, as he and Dooley had planned, he'd be back to life. Or back to . . . undead? I'm not sure the proper term."

Commissioner McManus took the vastsack, holding it as gingerly as a live grenade. He went to his desk and pulled out an old wool flat hat. He dumped the contents of my vastsack into the hat (which must have similar storage capabilities).

"Roscommon Football Club? I'm a fan myself," said the commissioner as he handed me back my vastsack.

Finbar Dowd tapped the flat hat with an old iron horse-shoe, and a little bit of faerie magic rippled over it, sealing up Crom Cruach inside, then passed the hat to the commissioner, who put it on, just like an ordinary hat that did not have an undead bog mummy inside of it.

"The Secret Sheerie Service and I will deliver Crom Cruach to the National Museum in Dublin this very afternoon. They're expecting us. Of course, the return of the

Bog Man means that your parents will be exonerated, their records expunged. I have confirmation of that from my counterpart in the human administration," said Commissioner McManus.

"Very good news indeed," I said, "but as the covert operative Figs had told me, my parents escaped from Mountjoy and their whereabouts are currently unknown. After I arrest Dooley, I must find them. I'm worried sick."

"A bit more clarification on that: Yes, your parents escaped from Mountjoy prison. Your mum and da had heard a rumor on the inside that you had fallen into Dooley's clutches, and their escape was part of an ongoing effort to rescue *you*."

"So they've gone after Dooley as well?" I asked

"It seems so. We were tracking them, and both Log and your folks were all converging on a likely spot that Dooley was headed to in Limerick. But before our agent could strike, he was attacked and nearly killed," said the commissioner with a grave look.

"Perhaps he should hear it from the horse's mouth?" said Captain de Valera.

"I'm not sure he can make himself a horse anytime soon, after whatever the Prince of Limerick did to him," said the commissioner as he ran his hand gently over the chimpanzee with wings that was asleep on his desk.

And like a true eejit, only then did I realize that the winged chimp was wearing a familiar hat. This little hero asleep in the dog bed was none other than my friend: Special Unit Undercover Púca Horatio Fitzmartin Dromghool!

"Figs!" I gasped as I rushed to him and stroked his wee furry head. He was in quite a state, feverish, unable to see, and his face speckled with a bit of . . . *glitter.*

"Figs has been a champion, Ronan. After delivering me back here, he became a crow and went out to track your parents, and if possible, locate Cadet Log MacDougal as well," said Captain de Valera.

"Everyone was closing in on Lord Desmond Dooley," said the commissioner.

"Dooley's got Log's parents in a Prada vastsack of his own. We must rescue them as well!" I said. "Also, I would be remiss if I did not mention: Rahgnall, King of the Leprechauns, has offered me a closet full of gold and platinum shoes if I return Dooley to stand trial in Oifigtown."

"And I'm sure you refused, Boyle," said the commissioner. "On a few occasions, we've had Special Unit officers enter into illegal contracts with that little potato-shaped weirdo."

"If you think regular leprechaun gold comes with a curse, imagine what an entire closetful of gold and gems belonging to the most powerful leprechaun in all of mythology would do to you," said Siobhán, remembering some specific horror.

"One of our officers took a pair of sandals from Raghnall, with the promise they would make him famous. Do you know the Post Office Building in central Dublin?" said the commissioner.

"The famous one? From the 1916 uprising? With the bullet marks in the front?" I asked.

"Yep. That one," said McManus. "That's Ronald. He was a solid detective. Worked for my predecessor's predecessor. Ronald made a deal with Raghnall, took the sandals, and sure enough, now he's famous."

"He's a famous building?" I asked, now rocking Figs like a baby.

"Yes. Classic shenanigans. Want to be famous—poof, congrats: Now you're a famous building. That's why we don't trifle with the wee folk, Boyle," said the commissioner.

"Will Figs be all right?" I asked as I stroked his sweaty, glitter-covered chimp brow.

"He's on the mend," said Captain de Valera. "But slowly. He's in an induced sleep for now, until his shape-shifting settles and he can become one specific animal again. Sergeant O'Brien's been quite helpful, as she understands the needs of a púca folk."

"Who did this to him?" I asked, my rage growing.

"The Prince of Limerick," said Captain de Valera, furrowing her brow with an anger that paired well with matte black lipstick.

"Who is this prince? Another wee royal? Whoever he is, I'll kill him," came out of my mouth as I lifted Figs up and kissed the chimp head under his famous hat.

"The Prince of Limerick is not faerie folk," the commissioner explained. "He's a human like us. At least he *was* a human at some point. Now, I cannot say for sure. He's more evil than anything you've encountered yet, and yes—I'm counting Crom Cruach. He is also Lord Dooley's benefactor."

"Log and your parents had both separately managed to track Dooley to the prince's castle in Limerick. Your parents by using their contacts in the art world, and Log by shaking down every talking rabbit and butter churn from here to Gweedore," said Finbar Dowd.

"Dooley is an art thief, but he's funded by a master of deception—an unscrupulous overlord with unlimited resources—the Prince of Limerick."

"The prince is as rich as twenty sultans. He lives in the castle called Lisnacullia, up in Limerick," said Captain de Valera as she flipped Lily on her back beside the peat fire and gave her some professional belly rubs. "Lisnacullia lay in ruins for five hundred years until the prince reinstalled himself there. He's been pouring his riches into it, restoring the tower, making it a real fortress once again. He's also been stuffing Lisnacullia with pilfered treasures—relics of the human and faerie realms, curated and acquired by his 'bestie,' Lord Desmond Dooley."

"Figs tracked Log and Rí to Lisnacullia, where they had caught up with Dooley. But Figs had arrived in his crow form and was about to become a chimpanzee when the castle's SDS system attacked him, sending three thousand volts of electricity into his little púca body," said the commissioner, becoming sadder and more handsome by the minute.

"SDS?" I asked.

"Smart Defense System," said Finbar Dowd. "Figs has lost his shapeshifting power for now . . . hopefully not forever."

"The prince is as paranoid as he is rich. He's obsessed with security. Lisnacullia's defense systems were installed by the same folks who did the Large Hadron Collider at CERN," said the Commissioner.

"Yikes," I said because that was the best my Brian could come up with.

"The prince boasts that because of this defense system,

Lisnacullia is impenetrable," said Captain de Valera, who was massaging Lily's paws "I don't believe that. Hard to get in? O'course. Impossible? *No*."

"Log and Rí are held captive inside that castle?" I asked. "Let's go. I'll rid us all of this troublesome prince myself."

"Indeed, the prince has Log and Rí captive. And Dooley is thought to be holed up in there as well. The prince and Dooley are plotting some major caper. Figs was in bad shape when he got back, but he was able to scribble out a few details."

"Limerick is less than two hours away. I can leave right now."

"You'll need to see the Mysterious Doctor Boiko first. Have your wounds and obvious brain damage tended to. Water and ice cream for the wolfhound, Mr. Dowd, and see that her pads are soothed with balm," said the commissioner to the little man whose face is impossible to remember.

"O'course, Commissioner," said that guy.

"Boyle, the Prince of Limerick is prepared for us. In fact, before Figs collapsed, here's what he wrote . . ."

Commissioner McManus handed me a note that was obviously written by a pen in the mouth of a dazed chimpanzee. What I could make out was:

LISNACULLIA CASTLE
LOG AND RÍ CAPTURED
DOOLEY AND PRINCE TO [ILLEGIBLE] RONAN BOYLE

"We've tried lots possibilities," said the commissioner. "The best we've come up with is LURE or KILL for the missing word."

"Oh," I said with a thud.

"Yes, it's likely that Dooley and the prince are trying to lure you to Lisnacullia," said McManus.

"Then we should oblige him," I said, acting like the teenage bad boy persona I was trying to cultivate.

"That's why you won't be going alone; you'll have the captain as well," said the commissioner.

Captain de Valera stood and stretched, pulling her vinyl boot surprisingly close to her own head.

"Not just me," said the captain, kicking her other leg

up and stretching it like some sort of Russian circus/ballet person. "You'll have a fellowship: myself, Lily, Tim, and our secret weapon, Yogi Hansra."

"That's predominantly ladies," I said doing some quick math. "Shouldn't we call that a ladyship instead of a fellowship?"

"Good point," said the captain, nodding. "You'll have a ladyship of the first order. And of course, Tim, who has turned out to be a pretty useful bear and was recently promoted."

"Get out of that moldy beret and see Doctor Boiko at once. You'll rendezvous with the ladyship at the port cochere within the hour. Your friend Log MacDougal is counting on you, Boyle. So am I," said the commissioner.

I put Figs back in the dog bed and gave his head a good sniff, in case I needed to remember him.

"Rest now, Figs," I whispered to him, "this prince will rue the day he trifled with us."

Chapter Eleven

NEW SHILLELAGH, WHO DIS?

The Mysterious Doctor Boiko—who is not a medical doctor but rather an occult witch doctor from the spookiest forests of Romania—gave me a physical and mental tune-up in his macabre exam room. Part of his astonishingly brief treatment was having me drink five room-temperature pints of a fetid soup he called "The Sting of Mycenae!" I assumed this was some elixir of the ancient Greek city of Mycenae, given to their Olympians or their warriors before battle or some such magnificence.

But sometimes M.D. Boiko's accent is tough to decipher,

and I realized when he pointed to his assistant (who looked just like a little version of himself) that he was actually saying "This thing of my son, Andy."

So the broth, while not a gift of the ancient Mycenaeans, was made by the doctor's son, Andy.

The first four pints had no discernible effect other than seven trips to the bathroom. But as the last trickles of the fifth pint were forced into my esophagus in a painful GULP, a tingle of energy blasted through my nervous system, from my toes up to my BRAIN. Where my bum and shoulder had been poked by mythical weapons—those spots were now just itchy. *So* itchy, and then numb, then remarkably better! This "Thing of My Son Andy" had made my body's healing process condense to a few seconds. As a bonus: My nasal passages—which human doctors have diagnosed as "barely usable," "oh dear," and at "fifteen percent" capacity"—were suddenly dilated, flooding my head with oxygen.

A few minutes later, I was in the Supply and Weapons Department, where the eyes of the Work–Release Troll on duty went wide when I handed him my emergency supply order signed by the commissioner himself.

"OOOOOH. The 'misshy 'imself says you need the state-of-the-art rig, eh?" said the troll. "Gimme a coupla minutes, luv. And you'll want to keep this, I'd imagine."

She tossed me the medal from my old jacket and started passing me new items through the opening in the chicken wire cage.

"Let's see here," said the troll as she pulled the trigger on a barcode scanner, *beep, beep*ing up my new supplies: "Adult men's kilt, small; jacket, extra narrow; socks, narrow; waterproof boots, 42 narrow; and oooh, very nice . . . NB4 shillelagh? Oooh, what are ye up to, boyo? What would the narrow boyo need an NB4 for? I'll need a supervisor to get that from the back."

She ducked into the back with a concerned look on her trollface. I stepped into the changing room and put on all of my new gear, which, combined with the pints of elixir, made me feel brand-new. I could overhear a brief exchange between the troll and the human supervisor in the back, and when I emerged in my new rig, the troll had returned, holding a sleek box and clipboard with a stack of legal paperwork.

"An NB4 shillelagh requires signing these release forms," said the troll.

"O'course," I said. "But I'm actually not sure what an NB4 shillelagh is?"

"Noggin Banging, Category 4," said the troll with respect. "It's the lightest possible blackthorn root, with the hardest possible headstock. The deadliest shillelagh yet made. Not for noobsters."

She opened the box, and I couldn't help but gasp when I saw the new fighting stick that lay inside it. The stem was forty inches long, with tiny spikes all the way up. The wood was so black that it seemed to be ebony. The headstock was carved into the face of an angry harpy with a protruding beak that gave the stock the added use of also being a hook.

"Can I hold it?" I asked like some kind of eejit.

"I certainly hope so, it's yours," said the troll. "Careful where you swing an NB4, boyo, it's not a toy."

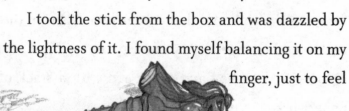

I took the stick from the box and was dazzled by the lightness of it. I found myself balancing it on my finger, just to feel its sublime evenness. The tip of the harpy's beak, while a terrific hook, was also as sharp as a diamond.

"The hook's made from synthetic unicorn horn," said the troll as she followed my eyes. "Sharper than a diamond, and more humane than cutting off an actual unicorn horn, which folks frown on these days—EVEN THOUGH THERE IS A SURPLUS OF UNICORNS IN TIR NA NOG AND THOSE WHO 'HARVEST' A FEW ARE REALLY DOING ALL OF US A FAVOR," added the troll, regurgitating some facts from a popular faerie folk podcast called *Wurst of Times*.

(When mythical folk quote *Wurst of Times*, which spews dangerous radical faerie beliefs, you can pretty much assume that they are a follower of the Late Queen Moira with the World's Most Interesting Forehead. She was the wee royal who wanted to annex the human realm and turn us into sausages. *Wurst of Times* is a pox on human/faerie relations and is really just a way to get faerie folk to buy a bunch of pre-packaged spells that the hosts of W.O.T. hawks between vitriol-filled monologues.)

"Now I just need your autograph on these consent forms, saying you're aware that this is an NB4, and that you've been trained, and will not hold the clurichaun who made it legally responsible for injuries or deaths caused by the stick, yadda yadda . . ."

I signed my name in thirty-five spots on the paperwork, which she passed through the chicken wire. While I barely skimmed the text of what I had just signed, part of it seemed to imply that I had just agreed to arbitration with some clurichaun, rather than a lawsuit, in the event that I did something terrible with this shillelagh.

Hopefully these legalities would never come up.

The troll passed me a few accessories that clicked to my belt, including a weaponized pickle juice atomizer and an antidote tablet to crack under my tongue in case of a love spell. Then a new sporran, pre-loaded with mints and tissues, sock flashers, and a book of weapons-grade dirty limericks to distract the wee folk. And then, best of all, because I had an emergency supply order from the commissioner: Everything was forty percent off.

I was tempted to purchase a new vastsack, but perhaps

the Roscommon Football Club one had brought me good luck so far. I decided not to mess with that.

The ladyship was assembled at the port cochere when I arrived. Yogi Hansra was leading everyone through a few of her famous "hip opener" stretches and I silently joined in.

Captain de Valera pulled up in one of the Special Unit Jeeps, which are so well camouflaged that they become almost invisible to the naked eye. If they weren't ever so loud, you'd likely not know they were there. This one had the gold license plate featuring a harp and the number 7, the very same vehicle that the captain had at Clifden Castle so many Wednesdays ago, when I went down an oubliette and got this low-paying-yet-exciting job.

As Yogi Hansra popped up from her pigeon pose, I shook hands with her, and of course she took that opportunity to disarm me, taking away my brand-new shillelagh and pinning me to the ground, her knee dropping right onto the softest part of my neck.

"When is shillelagh training happening, Boyle?"

"Always . . ." I rasped. "The past, the present, the distant future."

"Then why have you given me such a perfect chance to overpower you?"

"BE . . . CAUSE . . . I AM AN EEJIT."

"Excellent. You were an eejit today, but you don't have to be one tomorrow."

Yogi Hansra hoisted me back to my feet and returned my new shillelagh to me.

"Good to see you, Tim," I said to the medium-sized bear who was scratching his furry back against one of the pillars that support the port cochere. "How's, um . . . how are you doing, man?"

(I would regret the fact that I said "man" to Tim, who is so clearly a bear, for many years to come.)

It didn't seem like Tim understood my words. He simply sharpened his terrifying claws on the stone steps, then bounded off, disappearing into Killarney National Park and in a northernly direction, which luckily was the way toward Limerick.

"Tim doesn't like to ride in the Jeep. He gets carsick, then he starts chewing things with his teeth," said the captain as we loaded into the vehicle.

Yogi Hansra rode shotgun, I was in the back with Lily as we zipped along the N21 toward Limerick.

"Some light reading on the prince," said the captain as she tossed me a thick file labeled CLASSIFIED.

My mouth went through the stages of disbelief—slack—stunned—jaw on the floor—as I read the prince's file.

"Can this be right?" I asked.

"Yes," said the captain.

"So the Prince of Limerick is . . . no . . . it cannot be him? It's *that guy*?" I shook my head, dropping a few pages of the file onto the floor.

Yogi Hansra nodded to me in the rearview mirror.

"But . . . he's famous. It can't really be him? Everyone loves him. I mean, I don't, but my mum and da do. I always thought he was a bit of a cheeseball."

"Never meet your heroes, Ronan," said the Yogi.

"Oh, again: He's not my hero—he's quite the cheeseball. I just can't see how this man is the Prince of Limerick."

"Because he's so very well-known, and because of the state-of-the-art security system at his castle, we'll try to gain entry *without* the use of force," said Yogi Hansra.

"So, we'll sneak in? Unseen? *To this guy's castle?* Impossible."

"Oh, we'll be very seen," said the Yogi. "We'll fight with a mirror instead of a big stick."

"We'll be hiding in plain sight," said Captain de Valera with a smile, her matte black lipstick underscoring the level of quiet confidence that she radiates.

"I'm sorry? We're using mirrors or some such? I must have missed the explanation of the plan," I said, confused.

Yogi Hansra often speaks in poetic nuance, in order to make the listener figure things out for themself.

"Oh, Boyle, you've been using brute force out in the field for too long. You must unremember some of your instincts. Remember, instead, the young Greek Narcissus. Narcissus was told he would live forever, as long as he never saw his reflection. But then what happened to him, Boyle?"

OH JEEZ. *Here we go.* I had forgotten how exhausting it can be to spend time with Yogi Hansra, who is always doing a bit of Yoda-type stuff with me (when she's not straight-up hitting me with sticks or her elbows).

"Narcissus saw his reflection in a river and he could never look away. He pined there, in love with his own face, until he died," explained the yogi as if this would make our plan clear to me, which it did not.

"The Prince of Limerick is our Narcissus, Ronan," said the captain. "If you've read that file, you'll see his main weakness is how much he fancies himself. We'll hide the Jeep a short distance from the castle and get into our disguises. If we play it cool, we'll capture Dooley, rescue Log and Rí, and be in Limerick at the Chicken Hut for a nice gravy by nightfall!"

The captain's speech was inspiring, despite the fact that both Yogi Hansra and I are vegetarians and that the notion of a hut filled with chickens is a nightmare.

Chapter Twelve
AER LINGUS IN-FLIGHT CHANNEL NEWS CREW

A short while later, Enid, a young reporter with the looks of a Bollywood movie queen, Kurt, a handsome cameraman with an ironic handlebar moustache and matte black lipstick, and an emotional support wolfhound named Siegfried 2.0 were standing at the high-security portcullis of the once-ruined, now-revamped castle known as Lisnacullia.

With them was a narrow, young segment producer for the Aer Lingus In-Flight Channel named Doris Toil.

A little detail about this group: None of them were

affiliated with the national Irish airline Aer Lingus! Nor the Aer Lingus In-Flight Channel! Enid was not named Enid, and Kurt had matte black lipstick on because he was, of course, Captain Siobhán de Valera in disguise. This so-called news crew was, in fact, a Trojan horse!

I was playing the role of the ever-so-hip segment producer Doris Toil, and Lily was pretending to be an emotional support animal named Siegfried 2.0 (not really a stretch for her). Somehow, the captain even had Aer Lingus bags and boxes, in which to hide our Special Unit gear.

I had flipped my kilt around so that the pleats were in the front, which, while completely bonkers, made it look like I was wearing a skirt. Captain de Valera also provided me with sunglasses and a bright pink bob wig that she said was from her "karaoke drawer."

I will skip the bit about the captain helping me into a wig of hers—that even smelled like her—and how that made me feel like I was floating above my own life, like some sort of Brian Bean made out of soda pop fizz, while I got lost in her two-color eyes. But I have never left out details, however embarrassing, from these journals, which I have no idea what I'll actually do with anyway. Maybe I'll just mail them to them to *whatshisface* the Deputy Commissioner when all of this is done?

Anyway, I guess I tell you as a warning. If your own face is ever a few inches from Captain Siobhán de Valera—*and I don't care who or what you are*—part of you will want to go live in those two mismatched eyes of hers. It's just science.

Moldy old Lisnacullia towered over us like a . . . well, a tower. You get it. The place was built in the fourteen or fifteen hundred-and-something-and-somethings, by the McSheehys, who were famous for being "difficult." That they were kind of "a lot" is a historical fact, and not me throwing shade at them because they happened to be Scottish mercenaries, imported to Ireland because of how much they loved to bonk people on the head with sticks. One of my best mates, Gary, is both Scottish and a werewolf. There's really nothing wrong with those wonderful Scots that you couldn't fix by simply *hiding the Irn-Bru* someplace they won't find it.

This new Lisnacullia remodel was tricked out with

state-of-the-art additions: solar panels (in ever-cloudy Ireland? sure), a half-dozen satellite dishes, and a huge conservatory on one side, with its glass steamed up—implying that it must contain an indoor swimming pool.

The "prince" of this castle would never agree to being questioned by officers of the Special Unit of Tir na Nog. But he might gladly agree to three hours of superficial on-camera chit-chat with a popular airline in-flight entertainment channel.

Narcissus was an understatement.

On the other side of the portcullis, in this high security castle, we were about to meet one of Ireland's sparkliest living cheeseballs. A man so dripping with schmaltz that he leaves a trail of it wherever he frolics.

"Air Lingus In-Flight Channel News Crew and our emotional support dog," announced Captain de Valera, dropping her voice down convincingly as she spoke into the security camera at the portcullis. "Here to interview the prince for that profile for our in-flight channel."

There was an epic pause. (Had we been unmasked before our caper even began?) Then a pleasant female voice responded from the other side of the little blue lens, which blinked, batting like an eyelash.

"Welcome to Lisnacullia. Please stand back while the portcullis retracts and I'll meet you inside in the foyer."

Our fictional news crew resisted the urge to smile as the metal gate rose, and we waltzed right in to the most secure castle in this part of Limerick, in this part of Europe, in this part of the world, about to arrest Lord Desmond Dooley.

The portcullis groaned shut behind us, sealing us inside with a heavy metal *CLOONNNG*. The foyer was a compact stone hallway, designed to be small so any medieval intruders could be swiftly decapitated if they made it beyond the portcullis. One modern oddity about this castle was the strong smell of chlorine, which must have been coming from the indoor pool area. To our right, a spiral staircase led up into the tower, marked with a rope warning: ABSOLUTELY NO ADMITTANCE!

The owner of the voice from the intercom appeared,

surprising us by not being a person, but rather a state-of-the-art vacuuming robot—a shiny black disk on wheels, who zipped around our feet with pleasant *whirrrrrrrs* and *boooops*.

"Hi, I'm NORA. And I'm not just a vacuum, I'm a NEURAL OPERATING ROBOT ASSISTANT. N.O.R.A. Welcome to [bizarre pause] Lisnacullia Castle. Come into the treasures room and the master of the house will be with you shortly," she said in an overly flirtatious voice that wouldn't be appropriate for most workplaces.

Lily gave a curious sniff at the little robot, making a displeased furrow of her brow.

"I'll just need to see your identification," said NORA as she lit us with a little blue beam that blasted from her center.

We each pulled out our counterfeit news credentials, which had been done in stunning detail (I'm guessing by a leprechaun on work-release at Collins House).

NORA's blue light scanned the bar codes of the IDs and then across our faces with a little electric *hiss* that made my pupils contract.

After a stressful pause where she must have consulted with the castle's security system, she did a deft little U-turn and zipped out of the foyer with a cheerful ping.

"CREDENTIALS APPROVED. Right this way! And remember: I'm not just a vacuum! I'm a lifestyle assistant. Please do not touch ANYTHING in the castle, and never EVER leave the group. All of the upper levels of the castle are OFF LIMITS TO GUESTS," said the vacuum, sounding more threatening than she had a moment before. "NEVER, EVER GO EXPLORING IN THE CASTLE. GUESTS WHO STRAY IN THE CASTLE WILL BE DEALT WITH SWIFTLY, AND HARSHLY. [bizarre pause] I can also play your favorite podcasts like *Wurst of Times!* and *The Daily*."

NORA sprayed a bit of mist in the air. At first I thought it was air freshener, until it passed over us and it burned our faces and hands—it was something to sanitize us.

"The prince has many irreplaceable Irish treasures on display, and we like to keep germs off of the relics."

"NORA, we'll need a place to set up our equipment for our In-Flight Channel interview," said Yogi Hansra, not altering her voice at all, as apparently she didn't need to do so because she was *totally plausible* as some sort of hip reporter.

"I am processing that right now. Did you know that I'm not just a vacuum? You can say things like: 'NORA, tell me a story.' Or 'NORA, what's a good gingerbread recipe?' If I get stuck, just pick me up and set me in a new location."

Our ladyship was already VERY over this annoying robot, who did veer off course several times to vacuum up lint and dust bunnies, proving that she was mostly just a vacuum.

NORA led us into a great hall where a peat fire played on a curved, high-definition television screen. I had only seen a curved TV screen of this magnitude once before, on a summer trip to London, on the fourth floor of Harrods department store next to a ONE-PERSON SUBMARINE. So—yes—the owner of this castle had television that is in the SAME PRICE CATEGORY AS A MINI SUBMARINE.

Enough stolen loot to fill a small museum was displayed around the room: something that looked like the actual

Book of Kells; a spear made for a giant that seemed to be hewn from the bone of a sea monster; and beside it, the skeleton of a dog the size of a rhinoceros. A tag below them read: ACTUAL SPEAR AND HOUND OF CÚ CHULAINN—A GIFT FROM LORD DESMOND DOOLEY.

"Grrrrr," said both Lily and myself as we looked upon these treasures that had no business being inside a private castle with a built-in spa somewhere giving off a chlorine smell. Of course this type of castle-owning weirdo was the sort of person lord desmond dooley would sell Ireland's greatest treasures to.

The walls were crammed with bric-a-brac and cheap magazine covers, some of which looked authentic and some of which looked like the kind of wacky photos that you can take at an amusement park, the ones where you could put yourself under the caption dreamiest bachelor alive.

The far side of the room was an entire Irish pub, down to the last detail. It seemed for all the world like a real pub, which must have been ripped clean out of its original spot in some little town and shoved by force into this monstrous room of treasures. Beside the pub was displayed a huge stone head that looked like it belonged in a museum, and parked beside that, a black Trans Am muscle car that was without a doubt from the 1980s. I drifted toward the stone head, which had a plaque identifying it as Head of Crom Cruach, Bronze Age. Having met, captured, and poked the actual Crom Cruach with my nice umbrella, I can tell you the resemblance was excellent. The Trans Am had a plaque identifying it as one of five original vehicles from the television show *Knight Rider* (twentieth century). The high/low aspect of the collection in this room proved something that Mum and Da had always told me: There's no accounting for taste, especially when it comes to rich people.

Some sort of smart exercise bike that looked like it could take flight and chase Will Smith around in a futuristic movie battle was perched in the middle of the room, making it absolutely certain that the person who decorated this hall, in a jumble of priceless treasures, workout equipment, and a car from *Knight Rider* was a genuine psychopath.

"Wow, banger of a room, mate. CRIKEY," I said,

completing my disguise with my very best Australian accent, for reasons unknown even to me.

Yogi Hansra and the captain both shot me panicky looks: *Australian accent? Seriously, Ronan? Can you maintain that? Bad idea!*

Honestly, I had not thought through this part of my Doris Toil disguise. I just went with it, and now this fake Australian accent was a bell that I could not un-ring. I guess some part of me thought it would go well with the pink wig.

"Real CROC'A-DOODLE-DINGO of a rumpus room, mate," I doubled down, like some sort of Australian mental case, loopy on ginger beer and dizzy from days in the out-back. Why was I making up fake Australian slang? We may never know.

"Was someone talking to me? HELLO!" moaned a voice from the middle of the room.

"NOBODY'S EVER TALKING TO YOU, PEPE," snipped NORA the vacuum, at which point I realized it was the exercise bike that had joined in the conversation.

"I'm sorry about PEPE, he's the PERSONAL

ELLIPTICAL PILATES EXPERIENCE. He's just an exercise bike and nobody's ever talking to him. They're talking to me, NORA, and I'm way more than just a vacuum."

"I'm actually a few things as well," moped PEPE bleakly. "Certainly yes, I am a state-of-the-art Pilates bicycle. But I'm also a friend in your corner and a scale that can measure your body fat."

"Those seem diametrically opposed," chirped NORA flirtatiously.

"Imagine being the most advanced Pilates bicycle in the world and never moving from this spot," said PEPE with the laconic ennui of some sad cat on TikTok.

The air hung heavy with a digital chill. Clearly, there was a pretty bad vibe between the smart vacuum and the smart exercise bike, and our fake news crew had unwittingly stepped right into the middle of their electronic grudge.

"If PEPE will shut up for a minute I can get back to my many jobs, because I am so much more than just a vacuum and really PEPE is an exercise bike that thinks you're too fat for your height," griped the little vacuum as cheerfully as a random von Trapp child while throwing shade at the bicycle, who actually seemed nice, if somewhat misunderstood.

PEPE the bicycle's sulk hung over the room like a bad Wi-Fi signal at a one-star internet cafe. Almost no one noticed when he started singing "Fields of Athenry" to himself in a laconic sotto voce that made even me, the fictional Doris Toil, want to unplug him.

We started setting up our "pretend television crew" gear. Spoiler alert: Under their disguises, everyone was armed to the teeth (except for Lily, who was armed *with* teeth). Between Yogi Hansra and the captain, we had the two best living shillelagh fighters in the world, and their fighting sticks were tucked in among the news gear, as was my brand-new NB4.

"NORA, tell me about your owner, the human of the household," said the captain, making small talk as she subtly consulted a shenanogram, checking to see if there was faerie mischief happening in the castle. The shenanogram went berserk, pointing back toward the spiral staircase, the one labeled ABSOLUTELY NO ADMITTANCE.

"I found something on the web for 'NORA, tell me about your owner.' Would you like to hear it?"

"YES," said the captain in that quietly furious tone in which humans started to speak to smart devices back in 2020.

NORA did a little loop, corralling our feet like a cowpoke to keep us on a path like so many "doggies."

"Seamus McSheehy is the Prince of Irish Dancing. His hit shows *TIP TAP TO TIPPERARY, POP TO CORK FOR NEW YEARS,* and *YOU GO YOUR WAY, I'LL GO TO SLIGO* have sold out theaters around the world and sold millions of tickets and home videos. *HELLO MAGAZINE* called him 'one of Ireland's MOST OVER THE TOP dancers.' Seamus McSheehy's feet are insured with Lloyd's of London for fifty million euros, and he himself has petitioned with UNESCO to have his ankles declared an official WORLD HERITAGE SITE," said the little vacuum proudly.

"What a bunch of pure blarney. I hear that Seamus

McSheehy is just a simple Irish fellow, even if he does dance like a living god," chuckled a voice that oozed like imitation butter on a gluten-free muffin.

Seamus McSheehy, Prince of Irish Dancing, Living Human Cheeseball, had just arrived in the hall. His arm was cocked jauntily against a scale model of the castle we were currently standing in. His black silk shirt was open all the way to the navel. His face and belly were so freshly spray-tanned, it seemed the color might drip off of him right onto the floor. His soft tummy hung out just a bit over a rhinestone belt buckle that I could have sworn was engraved with the words *IT'S ME!* His face and arms were airbrushed with just a bit of glitter, and he wore an actual crown of golden laurels atop his combover hairdo.

Wow.

"Welcome to my little castle. Seamus McSheehy. Prince of Limerick—what a silly nickname. *Hello Magazine* made that up. I'm a wee bit of a dancer, maybe you've heard? But I am also your humble servant," he said, bowing his comb-overed head to his foot in way that I have never seen a man of his age even attempt. "Has NORA offered you a drink? I have an entire pub that I purchased from the town of Castlebar and moved right into this room. Everything's for sale if the price is right."

"No, she hasn't offered drinks yet, Mr. McSheehy," said the captain, slipping her shenanogram away deftly into her vastsack and giving Seamus a firm handshake.

"NORA! Libations for our guests!" said Seamus as he did an absolutely perfect pirouette, with more rotations that I was expecting from a man with such a jiggly belly. The two-inch heels of his black dance shoes shone like mirrors, blinding us onlookers as they cut through the air.

Seamus McSheehy was not just a "good dancer."

Seamus McSheehy has a superpower that is dancing. His leaps and spins defy the Earth's gravitational pull. When you see him dance, you will be inclined, as I was, to check for wires that must be lifting him to such stunning heights. And just as it looks like he's about to come down from one of his leaps—he turns some internal afterburner jets and floats even higher.

There was only one thing that could give a little spray-tanned human such powers: He had made some kind of deal with the devil. The devil in this case was Lord Desmond Dooley, whose pointy nose was hanging right there in the room, in a photo with Seamus at some sort of gala for sinister, well-connected weirdos.

"We'll skip the drinks," said the captain. "We'd love to get right to the interview, and then hopefully we can get some footage around the rest of the castle? The upper floors and such?"

"You want to learn all my secrets, eh?" said Seamus, with a wink that was both sleazy and threatening. "Everyone always wants to know: 'Seamus, how is it that you dance like a living god? Have you got a bathtub of changeling tears that you bathe in every night?' HOW RIDICULOUS AN ACCUSATION!"

I assure you, nobody was thinking that Seamus had a bathtub full of changeling tears. AT LEAST NOT UNTIL NOW. Now it was all I could think of.

"Well, I assure you, it's . . . not that. At all. How would

I even get changeling tears?" giggled Seamus nervously in a way that made it absolutely clear that bathing in the tears of changelings is one hundred percent something he really does. "My dancing's just a simple gift, perhaps bestowed upon me by the spirit of Terpsichore herself."

"Terpsichore! Greek Muse of Dance," said Yogi Hansra, showing off some of her deep trivial knowledge as she arranged the camera and an armchair for our "interview." "How about for the chat, you will sit here, and I'll be up here on a stool, something like this, n'est-ce pas?"

"Oh, lovely. Perhaps we can get the scale model of Lisnacullia in the shot as well? I've spent a zillion euros upgrading this dump. The folks who did CERN did a bang-up job on the security system, it's got some surprising tricks up its sleeve. Perhaps the young lady can move my wee castle into the shot?"

"CRIKEY," I said as my undercover character Doris Toil started to really take form.

As instructed, I moved the scale model of the castle into the shot, just behind the armchair where Seamus would sit. The little model was stunning in its detail, little lights on in the windows, moss on the hill outside—it must have cost a fortune.

The yogi then led Seamus McSheehy into a trap so elegant that only now did I fully understand it. She had set up a chair for Seamus, with a soft and pretty pink light aimed at it (some of our bags had actual TV equipment). The yogi had set the camera pointed down from a high angle, so that as Seamus looked at the camera, it would draw his face up, deaccentuating the creases of his neck, which had spray tan lines like the rings of an old tree.

As Seamus took his seat, the pink glow of the light made him look years younger and the piece de resistance of the trap came into play: Beside the camera, Yogi Hansra had placed a TV monitor, which could be seen precisely from where Seamus was sitting. As he sat in the chair, he was completely and utterly transfixed *by himself.*

Our Narcissus had a closed-circuit river to look into.

When Seamus first caught his eye in the monitor, the spark of true love passed over his face and left him breathless. You could almost hear Whitney Houston start singing in the background. I truly hope that one day someone looks at you the way that Seamus McSheehy, Prince of Irish Dancing, looks at himself on a monitor.

"Let's go all the way back to the beginning," said Yogi Hansra, which was my cue that she had Seamus in her trap, and the captain, Lily, and I could spring into action and emancipate our comrades in the upper part of the castle.

"Like a lot of Irish people, I was born in Chicago, Illinois," said Seamus in the world's vaguest Irish brogue.

"You were born in the States?" asked Yogi Hansra, cocking one of her Bollywood movie–star eyebrows.

"Yes, but I didn't like it very much, and so I moved to Ireland when I was quite young, which explains my authentic local accent."

"How old were you when you came to Ireland?"

"Just barely thirty-five and a half. I had just given up trying to be an actor in Indiana; that was a mess. I took a long look at myself and said: '*Seamus, get out of Indiana and change your name. Folks love Irish dancing. You've got the looks. Why not give it a go?*' And since Indiana and Ireland are about the same size, that made sense to me to try a new life over here."

The interview droned on in the background as the captain, Lily, and I slinked into the shadows of the hall. Seamus McSheehy was caught in a Möbius of self-obsession. The captain and I could have been wearing diapers and juggling flaming Chihuahuas and Seamus McSheehy wouldn't have noticed.

As we ducked out of the hall, the captain deftly picked up NORA and tucked her into a vastsack on her belt.

"Uh-oh, looks like I'm upside down, please move me to a new location . . ." was the last thing we heard NORA say as she disappeared into darkness.

PEPE the exercise bicycle lifted up his screen and *looked right at us*, and then did the most expressive thing I've ever seen a smart exercise bike do: He nodded his screen, tipping it on its hinge, saying silently but ever-so-clearly: *I GET IT. GO, MY FRIENDS.*

Lily, the captain, and I ducked back into the foyer and toward the ABSOLUTELY NO ADMITTANCE spiral stairs that lead up into the tower. A small but sinister security camera was pointed in a way that we could not avoid being seen by it if we were to attempt to cross its path.

"Watch out," I said, holding back Lily and the captain from the camera's view. "How will we get around it?"

"That's where Tim comes in," said the captain as she pulled out a walkie-talkie from her belt.

"Go for Tim," said a voice on the other end—a voice I had never heard before but knew must have belonged to Tim the Medium-Sized Bear.

"How's it coming on the roof?"

"I've shut off the main alarm, so it's only sending the signal to me now, even if it goes off, which it shouldn't. In a moment I'll cut the power to the backup system, and you should see the light on that camera in front of you go out. The castle lights will dim for a moment, but when they come back up, that will mean the entire system and the backup are disarmed and it's safe to start the operation. P.S.—you're welcome. Tim the Medium-Sized Bear at your service."

Things I did not know/possibly had forgotten:

1. Tim the Medium-Sized Bear can speak.

2. Tim had COME TO LIMERICK, JUST NOT IN THE JEEP.

3. Tim was some sort of technical wizard who was currently dismantling a security system.

4. Tim had been given a walkie talkie.

"Tim is a technical genius," said the captain, filling in the blanks on some of these new facts. "He's made it to the roof."

"Wow," I said, stunned. "He's so much of a . . . regular-sized bear, I just didn't know he was . . . so clever. At stuff? Also I forgot he was with us. Completely forgot."

"Well, he's quite shy, and he abhors violence, so he's become a real champion of the Special Unit's Cyber Division, which has been growing substantially of late. Also, he hates to ride in the Jeep and he bites the dashboard and it gets all spitty and gross, so we let him travel on his own, and he get reimbursed."

"Oh, sure," I said, feeling horrible that I had always judged Tim on his bear-ness and not on anything else about him. How often had I done that with folks who were not bears? Of course Tim might be great at computer stuff, just the same way I am great at . . . say . . . having allergies?

"The pink wig works on you, by the way," said the

captain, lightening the tension while our off-screen bear compatriot dismantled the alarm system.

"Any minute now," said Tim over the walkie, "couple little snips and twists, and . . ."

From the hall, Seamus's voice bellowed on to the yogi.

" . . . I supposed I've never married because I'm such a perfectionist! I mean, who would be a suitable bookend to me, a man who dances like a living god? Of course I've turned down offers! Thousands of them. I shan't name names because that's not my style but JLo, JLaw . . . so many of the J-dots have slipped into my direct messages, even though I deleted the messages so it would be impossible to prove . . ."

Even from a distance, Seamus's fake accent was like hearing spray cheese coming out of the can.

From the walkie-talkie came an excited whisper: "Now."

And the lights in the foyer dimmed, and the security camera blinked off. With a giddy rush, we bolted up the spiral stairs. My heart did a drum solo as we dashed up the tower in our fun disguises. Our plan was working so easily!

So, so easily.

And then it hit me.

Perhaps this had all happened way too easily.

Our plan had worked too quickly and without any of the classic sort of hindrances or complications. This kind of thing never happens to me. If things happened this easily, why would I even write them down?

I started to hyperventilate. Maybe we hadn't laid a trap. Maybe Dooley and Seamus had set a trap for us. Exactly as Figs had described might happen in his scribbled note. Isn't that what Figs had written? And wasn't it extra suspicious that Tim, a medium-sized bear, had, after a short bit of training, somehow disabled a security system that was installed by the folks who did the Large Hadron Collider at CERN? How had Seamus McSheehy—a man in the dancing part of show business—been fooled by some fun wigs and an ironic moustache?

At the second floor of the spiral stairs, we landed in a classic banquet hall. A massive table ran the length of the room. The walls were lined with tapestries that, upon closer inspection, looked like reproductions of magazine covers. To my left, a tapestry three meters tall had Seamus's face on it with the caption WORLD'S DREAMIEST BACHELOR.

Amongst the tapestries were a half-dozen mounted animal heads with antlers. As you might guess, Ronan Boyle, vegetarian, is not a "mounted animal heads on the wall" enthusiast, so I was extra confused about the information that my eyes were sending to my brain. It just didn't compute. I stammered:

"Those heads . . . *look*. The stuffed heads on the wall. They look like . . ."

"Mice," said Log MacDougal. "Huge mouse heads with fake antlers. It was the first thing we noticed, too. So, so creepy."

Standing there behind me was Cadet Log MacDougal, a near giant, raised by leprechauns, legitimate psychopath, and my very best friend in the entire world. She hoisted me in her tattooed arms and did a version of a kiss that she does, where she puts her entire mouth over your nose and blows IN. It's disconcerting, tacky, and hilarious, and I wouldn't have expected anything less from her.

My friend (and Lily's sibling) the gray wolfhound Rí was at her side, tail bopping like a fuzzy metronome. Log's little walnut-faced parents waddled over. I was surprised to see Dave with the Courage of a Minotaur and Mary with the Legs that Go on for Days, as they had been trapped in Lord Dooley's vastsack when he fled North Ifreann.

Log's wee parents hugged me around the knees, weeping hysterically (something the wee folk do when they are either very happy or very sad, so I was waiting for a bit more context).

"Ah, smells like good old Ronan Boyle got some new underwear!" said Dave, who cannot see.

"I wish I could have warned you. Going up the spiral stairs is a trap. We fell for it too, right when we got here," said Log. "That's how we got stuck here. Love the pink hair, by the way."

"Wait . . . the stairs are a trap? We've got to warn Yogi Hansra," said the captain. "She'll be headed this way any minute."

Just then, Yogi Hansra came running into the hall,

doing probably the best one-handed cartwheel I would ever see.

"Phase one complete. Seamus is still looking at himself on the monitor, and will be for the foreseeable future! You found Cadet MacDougal, excellent. Now let's bag Dooley and we're *nothing but taillights toward Limerick*," said Yogi Hansra. And then, as she is quite perceptive, a pall crossed over her face as she added, "What's with the giant mice heads on the wall?"

"Bad news," said Log. "That's just it: the mounted mouse heads. And the magazine covers on the wall. They're massive, right?"

"Ridiculously so," I said.

"Here's the catch, and you might want to take a deep breath so as not to panic," said Log.

The yogi led us all in one of her cleansing breaths, which requires breathing in for one second, while breathing out for ten. When we had finished, Log confirmed the horrible news.

"The mouse heads: They're normal size," said Log.

"But, if the mice heads are normal size, *then we would be...*"

I would never finish the other side of this ellipses, as just then, a booming voice shook the castle, as if the walls were made of balsa wood.

"HELLO, TINY EEJITS," said the nasal hiss of Lord Desmond Dooley, my nemesis.

"Yes, that's the bad news. Look out the arrow loops and our predicament will be quite clear," said Log.

We all turned and looked out the only windows of the banquet hall, which were loopholes (those narrow slits used to fire arrows from old castles).

What we saw outside the castle would make this go down as the worst Thursday of my life. Lord Desmond Dooley and Seamus McSheehy were looming down at us, waving hello like giddy lunatics. The worst part: They were 90 meters tall (about 300 feet). Somehow, they were standing in the hall of treasures, where we had left Seamus doing his interview.

"Wait, if Dooley and McSheehy are 300 feet tall, and

the mouse heads on the wall are regular size, that would mean . . ."

This ellipses I would finish, as soon as my poor brain could process it.

". . . that would mean that *we have become tiny*," I said, aghast.

"Exactly. That's the little surprise of the Security Defense System. *We're trapped in a scale model of the castle*," said Log.

"Not just any model of the castle, you stupid little weirdos," chuckled 90-meter-tall Seamus McSheehy. "You're in my replica of Lisancullia. Exact to the smallest detail. I believe the ugly pink-haired girl Doris even helped me move it, not ten minutes ago! Maybe next time, don't cross over a rope that says ABSOLUTELY NO ADMITTANCE! I TOLD YOU THE SECURITY SYSTEM HAS A LITTLE TRICK UP ITS SLEEVE!"

Giant Dooley and giant Seamus howled and cackled, giving each other near-miss high fives as if this was the funniest thing that had ever transpired. Behind them, I could see PEPE the smart bicycle, his screen drooping as if to say: *I'm so sorry.*

Doing a quick bit of math, I figured each of us (Log being the tallest) seemed to be now around 3 inches tall. I did not feel different in any way. My feet were still there, my glasses. I could feel all of my parts. Yet, I was, to be specific, about the size of a Princess Leia action figure, which meant that Log was about the size of a Chewbacca.

"'BUT HOW!?' RONAN BOYLE GASPED IN THE SHRIEKY LITTLE PARROT VOICE OF A NARROW EEJIT OF THE SPECIAL UNIT!" mocked the giant Lord Desmond Dooley, sticking his huge nose up to the loophole window of our little castle, doing a spooky laugh like the understudy in a regional production of *Dracula.*

"BEST SECURITY SYSTEM IN THE WORLD! SAME FOLKS WHO DID THE LARGE HADRON COLLIDER AT CERN!" bellowed Seamus McSheehy, who now rose above us like a spray-tanned Godzilla, flicking the castle with his finger just to frighten us. "I SAID IT WOULD NEVER WORK, BUT WE GET THE CERN FOLKS, AND

A BIT OF FAERIE MAGIC. THEN WE THREW SOME MONEY AT THE PROBLEM AND LOOK AT YER TINY STUPID FACES! WELCOME TO MY . . . *LITTLE* CASTLE. DO YOU GET IT NOW?!"

Dooley fell on the floor laughing. Seamus picked up the model of the castle and gave it a jiggle, which sent all of us tumbling and screaming like the dolls in a play set that we very precisely were.

Log tucked her parents under her huge, tattooed arms as we were rolled and tossed about the banquet hall as if we were in some kind of dry shipwreck.

"The model's made of balsa wood, quit yer whinge-ing, ye wee babies!" cackled Lord Desmond Dooley as he took the model from Seamus and flipped it upside down. "Softest wood in the world! And I believe this bear belongs to you as well?"

With another nasty shake of our model castle, Tim the Medium-Sized Bear tumbled into the hall—a jumble of technical gear strapped to his furry middle section. Tim, who had always been medium size, was now as small as the rest of us, or just slightly taller than Log.

"Oh, hello all. Bad news. Turns out if you try to bypass the security system, a sort of a spell kicks in to the whole castle." said Tim, telling us what we had just realized moments ago. "By my math I'm now about eight centimeters tall. Anybody else notice anything strange?"

"Yes, we're all a few centimeters tall, trapped in a scale model of the castle," I said, gesturing through the loophole to the 90-meters-tall humans who were giggling outside.

"Yikes," said Tim. "Major bummer. Sorry, everyone. I must say, it did seem like it was all going a bit *too* well."

"Trapped Ronan Boyle and his cohorts, and we're a half hour ahead of schedule," said Dooley with psychotic joy.

Dooley and Seamus did a gleeful little jig. Though I found him very annoying, I will admit that Seamus McSheehy was inarguably planet Earth's finest living dancer. Even a sarcastic victory jig from him is full of passion, precision, technical prowess, and joie de vivre, which proves that theory people are always saying, that the way you do something is the way you do everything.

"We're quite a pair!" said Seamus. "You supply me with

the treasures, the stolen faerie artifacts, and most importantly: the changeling tears. And in return, I give you the
cold, hard euros!"

"NOT TRUE! You give me much more than that, my
dear Prince Seamus. You give me a sense of accomplish-
ment. When we do our evil shenanigans together, I feel that
I am really making a difference in the world. The world of
evil mischief, *but still*."

"You're too kind, my Lord Dooley," said Seamus,
beaming at himself in a mirror behind Dooley. "And evil
mischief really is the best kind of mischief, am I right or am
I right?"

Seamus did a happy little soft-shoe routine as
Dooley crossed over to the (full-sized, stolen-from-the-
town-of-Castlebar) pub and poured them two pints
of stout.

"And now all of your many enemies are trapped by this
expensive scale model. And we move our plan to the next
level!"

Seamus toasted his pint glass, locking eyes with Dooley,
the sparkle turning sinister.

"Right, perfect. I get to kill Boyle and his mates, and then we'll do your thing," said Dooley.

"NO! You work for me, remember?" Seamus said. "I'm the one paying for all of these evil shenanigans. Remember your harebrained attempt to awaken Crom Cruach—REMEMBER HOW I SAID IT WAS A BAD IDEA AT THE TIME?"

"O'course, Seamus," hissed Dooley. "And ye've been lovely, and so generous with the purse strings! The Crom Cruach thing WOULD have worked without that narrow Boyle boy monkeying up the works.

"Seamus, relax. Of course, as I have promised: We're going to the Strangeplace, as planned. We'll dip your feet in the River of Balor."

"We dip my feet and make me a living god of dance. All of your stuff—revenge, killing your enemies— that stuff is TBD after I get what I want. You double-cross me, Dooley, so help me, I will leave footprints on your face so bad that yer own mum wouldn't recognize you," said Seamus, flexing his thighs menacingly, which is actually a thing he can do.

"You're all worked up, but you don't see how simple it is," Dooley said, simpering. "The river that we dip your feet into will kill humans or faerie folk who are dropped in it. So it's one-stop shopping! I throw my enemies in the River of Balor, same place where we dip your feet. It's all part of a promise I made to myself, and this was the year that I was NOT going to break promises to me."

"Why do we even have to bring them? The boy and his little gang trapped in the little model castle, for which I paid top dollar. Let's just throw the model into some regular river here in Limerick, and they'll drown, and we avoid all the hassle of bringing a bunch of random folks to the Strangeplace. There's probably an icky nasty river less than five minutes from here—I'll Google map it."

"THAT'S NOT THE PROMISE I MADE MYSELF, IS IT?!"

"Who cares? They're trapped in the model, with no escape, and if that's not cruel enough for you, we'll toss the model in a hole someplace and throw a few cow turds top of them. I can find you cow turds around here in ten seconds."

"NO! I promised myself that I'm throwing Ronan Boyle

into the River of Balor and that's what I'm doing!" screamed Dooley, sounding unhinged even for him.

Seamus sighed. "I just feel like it's overkill. It's a hat on a hat. That's the problem with you, Dooley. We could be out, dipping my feet, taking over Tir na Nog in a violent, ill-advised coup—and you have to junk it up with a bunch of pointless revenge stuff. Hat on a hat, mate."

"WILL YOU SHUT UP!" howled Dooley. "You're ruining the surprise. I was all excited to do a thing, where when we get to the Strangeplace, I say, 'Perhaps you remember your mum and da'—and then I toss them all in the River of Balor together. I've even concocted a fun little scavenger hunt of clues he'll have to figure out. Do you think I just roll out of bed and come up with evil plans? I don't. A lot of effort goes into this stuff. BUT NOW YOU'VE RUINED THAT, HAVEN'T YOU, SEAMUS?"

Dooley pouted, kicking his pointy shoe against the stone head of Crom Cruach, which must have hurt like heck, as a horrible hiss came from his nose.

"Look, I'm excited to have feet with the powers of a living god," Seamus continued in his Irish/Chicago accent.

"Obviously, Lord Dooley. And then, once that's settled, I'm stoked to help you with your coup-in-Oifigtown thing. But what puts a wrinkle in my bum is that even though I am the guy paying for all of this, I feel like you never listen to my ideas. Like simplifying this revenge thing."

"And I appreciate you, Seamus. I really do. I hate when we fight like this."

"You took a vow. And a lot of up-front money, Dooley. The river, then we do the violent coup, and then, the most important part of our plan . . . the real reason we're doing all of this . . ."

Seamus moved in toward Dooley. He had kicked off his dancing shoe and, without bending at all, placed a firm foot on Dooley's pointy shoulder, giving a threatening squeeze—yes, with his foot.

"Say it, Dooley. Say it out loud," whispered Seamus, hot blood pumping through his toes.

Dooley's lip quivered. Whatever nefarious thing was the last part of their plan, it made even Dooley uncomfortable to speak of it.

"Don't make me say it out loud, Seamus. It's not right."

"PRINCE OF LIMERICK, THANK YOU VERY MUCH. Until we're done, you call me by my official title, given to me by *Hello Magazine*, 2018. 'THE PRINCE OF LIMERICK,'" snarled Seamus, tightening the grip of his foot into Dooley's scant shoulder meat. "SAY. IT. YOU. MADE. A. VOW."

"Ow, ow, o'course. We dip your feet in the river. Kill King Raghnall in the coup. And then . . . we're going to . . ." —a bead of chilly sweat made a path down Dooley's marble face— " . . . and then . . ."

"SAY IT."

"And then we'll come back and get you some film work," Dooley blurted out, quickly, his face flush with shame.

"Yes. LEADING ROLES, too! None of this 'sidekick' rubbish. SEAMUS MCSHEEHY: PRINCE OF IRISH DANCING, STARRING IN FEATURE FILMS AND/OR NETFLIX SPECIALS," screamed Dooley as he pirouetted around the room with pure bloodlust in his eyes.

McSheehy's moves were stunning. Every spin with

perfect posture. His eyes could hit the exact same spot on each turn. Glitter radiated off of his spray-tanned belly like slow motion footage of the sun. At one point, for no reason other than showing off, Seamus set his pint of beer atop his head and continued to pirouette, never spilling a single drop.

"Yes, yes, my prince," said Dooley nervously. "It's just . . . just that . . ."

"JUST WHAT?" snapped Seamus, ending his spins with his foot back on Dooley's shoulder, causing Dooley to drop to one knee. "You don't like that part of our plan? That's the piece de resistance. It's the only reason we're doing this whole caper!"

"It's just that . . . the market for feature films about Irish dancing is well . . . I'm just not sure, in this new world that we inhabit, with so much competition . . . The Netflix special thing I get. That would make sense . . . maybe? But even so, are there outlets for Irish dancing movies starring a man of your age?"

A record-needle scratch was heard in parts of Iceland and beyond.

Dooley almost caught this faux pas before it farted out of his mouth, but not quite. Dooley had, in plain fact, just called Seamus McSheehy "too old to star in feature films."

The slow-motion slap that Seamus's foot made across Dooley's face would leave a mark that would never go away.

"Never speak to me like that again, Mister Dooley. Do we understand each other?"

For the second time ever, I saw Lord Desmond Dooley start to cry—and this time, he meant it. Dooley nodded his awful beak, whimpering, a bright red footprint on his cheek. The kind of permanent psychological damage that comes from being slapped by a pretty good friend stamped into his psyche forever. Not to mention being slapped by a foot.

"Don't make me do that again," Seamus said, cradling his foot to his chest. "These bad boys are insured with Lloyd's of London for fifty million euros. Not worth the deductible I have to pay if I break one on your stupid, pointy face, Dooley. Now, pack up your little enemies. It's showtime," said Seamus, throwing his pint glass into the peat fire (which was playing on a high-definition television screen, which, of course, meant that the glass and the HD screen shattered into a bajillion pieces).

Everyone gasped as glass rained down and mingled with the thin layer of glitter that already covered the floor.

"You work for me, Dooley—it's time that you remembered that."

"O'course, Seamus," whimpered Dooley like a dog caught in the rain. "Please don't foot-slap me again."

"WHAT? What did you just call me?"

"Sorry, yes your PRINCE-li-ness. Per *Hello Magazine*, 2018."

Seamus waited until Dooley actually took a knee, bowing like an actual servant of this tan prince of dancing.

"That's better. Now, YOU carry the model with your enemies. Because one: They're your enemies. TWO: It's heavy and I'm not in the mood and I think bringing them is a hat on a hat and we could skip it and dump them in a regular river."

Seamus McSheehy was out of the room like a gazelle, his toes only touching down twice to cover an area of at least twenty meters.

Dooley grumbled. He grabbed a tapestry off the wall and tossed it over the model, thrusting us into darkness.

"It's okay, Ronan, it's going to be okay," whispered Log.

"I don't think it is. We're about three inches tall, trapped in a scale model of a very nice castle. And he's going to dump us in some kind of river of death out in the Strangeplace!"

Your friend Ronan Boyle, like a lot of Irish people, is not afraid to cry. And right now, I was absolutely nailing a fierce Irish cry.

We rumbled along in the darkness. The huge table of the banquet hall had split right down the middle, as it too was made of balsa wood. The captain pulled a small torch from her belt, which illuminated our little mobile prison a bit. Yogi Hansra stepped over to me and adjusted my pink wig affectionately.

"Ronan Boyle. There are two ways to look at

our situation. One: Our ladyship is trapped, by enemies who are now fifty times our size, and there seems to be no remedy. Almost anyone who is on the outside who could help us is in here with us and we're going to be thrown in the River of Balor."

The yogi let that tragic update hang there, as she often does when making a point, and then she started stretching, the way she always does before a fight that she knows she is going to win.

"Or, Ronan Boyle, you could look at the situation more accurately. That you have ladyship with the two best shillelagh fighters in the world, two wolfhounds, two leprechauns, and a medium-sized bear. Plus Log MacDougal—genuine psychopath with the strength of two large bears . . . and Lord Desmond Dooley is taking us right to your parents."

In spite of ourselves, everyone gave a smile at the way Yogi Hansra presented our situation. While the yogi gets esoteric sometimes, she's also very good at seeing the forest for the trees or vice versa, however that expression works.

I suddenly felt well enough for an encouraging shout—somewhat muffled through my sobs.

"All right people, you heard the yogi, everybody hold on to something—it's gonna be a bumpy ride."

The yogi hugged me, pulling me out of Log's huge arms. It felt so nice, and almost stopped my Irish cry.

"Don't cry for us, Ronan Boyle—pray for Dooley and McSheehy," said Yogi Hansra with a mischievous sparkle in her almond eyes.

"Right, pray for them," I laughed, wiping some tears and snot off my face.

"And Boyle, think. We can't be eejits from here on. Why would I be hugging you? Have I ever hugged you? Is hugging something that Yogi Hansra does?"

Of course I realized too late that the Yogi Hansra had me in a jiujitsu grip. It was never a hug. Not her style. It was a lesson. With a tiny twist of her ankle, I was laid out on the balsa wood floor, my brand-new NB4 shillelagh slipping from my grip and landing in the yogi's hand with aplomb.

"When is shillelagh training happening, Boyle?" asked the yogi, a gentle heel on my throat.

"Always," I said, smiling. The yogi put my pink bob wig back on as Log hoisted me to my feet.

With a jolt, our little castle was hoisted off the ground. Presumably the model was in the boney hands of Lord Desmond Dooley, a man not known for his upper body strength.

The captain's flashlight skittered away, leaving us as just a group of tiny voices in the blackness, heading off toward the one area that has never been mapped by the Special Unit: the Strangeplace in the Boglands.

Chapter Thirteen
VACATION RENTAL BY PRISONER

he next few hours were precisely what it would be like to star in a castle disaster movie, where, for reasons that could probably be explained by the folks that made the *Sharknado* movies, a fourteenth-century castle has been yanked from Limerick by a shady art dealer the size of the Statue of Liberty. He then carelessly runs around with the little castle, treating the folks inside as if they're on the Cú Chulainn Coaster at Tayto Park (Ireland's largest roller coaster).

Sorry, that one was a long walk, I know. But I feel obliged to tell you of my adventures as I interpret them, even if that means you hear how some of the bizarre sausages are made inside my noggin.

If you're wondering if it hurt to fly around the floors, ceiling, and walls while your inner ears can never get a sense of balance and two massive wolfhounds HOWL in agonized harmony. . .

The answer is: *kind of.*

Honestly, the balsa wood walls of the wee castle were quite spongey, and at first, even a bit fun to bounce off of. The worst part was that we all got splinters while trying to hold on, and it became distressing to never know where "up" would be next.

Yogi Hansra led organized spider walks around the ceiling and walls as the castle rotated. This was fun the first few hundred times and looked a bit like a whole group of scary girls who crawl on ceilings in horror films were out for a stroll. And of course, because she's not going to waste an opportunity like this, the yogi found a way to make it into a core workout, where we were all spider walking and kicking out an opposite arm and leg every few steps.

Like many of the days of my life, it would have been better to not be in a kilt. Yes, as Dave with the Courage of a Minotaur pointed out, I was wearing new underwear. That said, I hadn't really been hoping that my underwear would become a major character in this part of our misadventures. I tried my best to hold my kilt down whenever the castle did a loop-the-loop, but eventually, this became a battle I would not win.

Just when the castle had settled on its side for a bit, Dooley gave it one last flip, sending me to the ceiling and back. My kilt landed fully over my wig, and Captain de Valera gave me an actual smack on the behind before she pulled my kilt down. This was one of those times where my brain bifurcates into a few possible scenarios:

Did the captain "spank" me as a reprimand? As if to say *keep your kilt down, you eejit?*

Or: Was it the kind of good-natured camaraderie that football players do after scoring a goal? Like *nice one, mate!*

Because of my social anxiety and my complicated feelings about the captain, I would worry/debate/replay this moment right up until the moment of my death, at which point I already know that I have an appointment to regret a terrible high five that I once gave to Yogi Hansra.

The model castle of our imprisonment finally settled into a steady plodding, with the distant sound of horse hooves coming through the tapestry.

"If my shenanogram is right, we're on the UpNog Stream of Whiskey. From there, it's a wee hop into Strange-place," said Captain de Valera as she put on some more matte black lipstick even though there was NO REASON FOR THAT other than to look awesome.

Tim entered, carrying a tiny suit of armor just about his size.

"I've done some exploring. Everything that's back in the real castle is here in the model as well," said Tim, "or rather: It's all here, but done in miniature. Pretty cool, eh?"

"The entire pub as well?" asked little Mary, licking her lips.

"Yes, but the pumps don't work," said Tim. "They put a

small version of everything, but it's all just toys and wood and such. Check it out," said Tim as he broke off the arm of the suit of armor, "just balsa wood."

"The main thing right now is that we stay focused," said Yogi Hansra. "We need a plan, so that we may strike when the opportunity arrives."

"I can't tell you what to expect in the Strangeplace," said the captain. "I don't think any beefie knows the history."

"I know a wee bit," offered Mary. "There's a few lepre-chaun musicals about the Strangeplace. The short version is this: There used to be loads of Irish gods. Not just Crom Cruach, who ye've met, the fella who demands human sac-rifice. There were some nice ones as well."

"Danu, Goddess of Nature, Balor, Lord of Destruction, Brigid the Healer. Dagda, who was benevolent and fun—the king of Hassle-Free Harvests and Tides and such, that was his actual title, which most folks have forgotten now," added Dave.

"And loads of magical cows and bulls. And some hounds as well, so don't feel left out," added Mary as she gave Lily a little pat on the head.

"For a tiny country, the human realm of Ireland goes through a lot of deities," said Yogi Hansra.

"Back in the day, there was huge battle between your beefie gods, Balor, Brigid, Danu et cetera, and some of the leprechaun gods," said Mary.

"Well, these powerful ladies must have whacked each other pretty dang hard, because at the end of their fight, they had punched a hole in the fabric of Tir na Nog," said Dave.

"Like a geata?" I said.

"No," said Dave. "The geatas are just ins-'n'-outsies, there's loads of those. This was different. This was a rip in the realms. A connection between Tir na Nog—the lovely land of us wee folks, and Tuatha dé Danann—the spooky land of the old human gods. The energy flowed out and became a river."

"The River of Balor?" I said, doing that thing where you ruin someone's story by filling in the last few words unintentionally.

"Well, yes. Next time let me say that bit, Ronan, it was kind of the whole thing I was building up to," said Dave.

"Sorry, Mr. MacDougal," I said, as I didn't mean to ruin his story, I was just genuinely excited.

"The River of Balor changed the landscape. Plants and trees that had once lived peacefully side by side in the Boglands pulled up their roots and started milling about and talking politics. Some of the trees would go on to form bands, others would try their hands at playwriting," said Mary.

"The energy from the river made birds and fish switch places, and then they didn't like it, so they made the water and the air switch places instead, and then they went back to being themselves," added Mary.

"Wait, *wha*?" said Tim.

"None of this makes sense," I said, looking befuddled, which is something I am great at.

"That's just it, lads and ladies—nothing makes sense in the Strangeplace," said Mary, in a serious tone.

"But it's not mischief, nor is it minor faerie goofin'; it's a crack in two magical realms. A river that the power of the old gods bubbles out of," said Dave, blinking his blurry eyes.

"The energy changes things, yerselves included," said Mary. "Yer mate's not wrong to think that dippin' his feet in it will give them some powers. Folks have tried that before."

"So you can try to be 'ready' for the Strangeplace if that sounds fun to you, but there's no way yer going to be, so I'd just relax. How do you prepare for a fart that goes backward? Yes, that is a thing that happens there. How do you tell a waterfall to knock it off with the tuba, then you realize: The tuba was playing the waterfall?"

"More questions than answers in the Strangeplace," Mary went on. "Like: Why is the mayor of the Strangeplace an old piece of cheese who ran on the slogan: NUDE, RUDE, WITH A BAD ATTITUDE?"

"A piece of cheese is the mayor?" asked Yogi Hansra.

"Yes. And he won with that bizarre slogan!" said Dave, emphatically.

"Forget everything you've ever *not* known about the Strangeplace. Forget everything you *do* know about yerself, but remember some of your Hits of the 2000s Music Trivia. Hold on to your bum, and don't sneeze or your brain might just float out your nose and fly away on a quarter note," whispered Mary, holding on to her huge daughter's arm like a baby koala bear on its mama.

"We'll never be ready, and we might get turned into cold Scandinavian appetizers, but there's no point worrying about horrors what hasn't happened yet, so let's get some rest for now," said Wee Dave.

Everyone curled up and tried to get comfortable as our balsa wood prison bounced around a bit like a disaster movie playing on, as it might, on the Aer Lingus In-Flight Channel.

The hot vapor of reasonably priced whiskey came wafting up into our scale model prison.

"We're on the Upnog Stream of Whiskey now, on the border of the Strangeplace," said the captain, checking her shenanogram.

"There's unicorns that will pull barges along on the river. The beefies must have rented one. That's how they'll go from here," said Wee Mary.

"Try to hold your nose, officers—unless you're part

leprechaun, this amount of whiskey fumes could cause permanent brain damage," said the captain.

I did a quick replay of the events of the past weeks that might have given me Brian's fromage (the real name of which I could still not remember. I know that it's whatever lizard they use when your Brian can't recumbent bicycle things any morgue). The hike in the Steeps, Laura the Cave Whale. The Second Queendom? There was zero chance I was coming out of this adventure in my right mind, no doubt about that. But this adventure had taught me something much bigger. Something I could never have learned in any book.

I look cool in a kilt and pink bob wig.

Sure, I had probably hurt the inside of my skull-stuff getting Brian's fromage. No time to worry about that now. Just time to sing all of Dermot Kennedy's "Giants" in my head. Which I did for several minutes, while I bopped my pink wig back and forth, enjoying the feeling of the faux bangs on my forehead. Perhaps my Brian area was actually lighter now? Felt like it. Felt goooooooood.

Log leaned in to me, with her classic concerned giggle

(the kind she did when she was saying something important, not funny).

"Ronan, ye all right, mate? You've been signing Dermot Kennedy's 'Giants' for a while now and it's a tad disconcerting."

I just smiled back, because I was so happy to be anywhere looking this awesome. When I started on this mission, before I'd killed off a few billion of my Brian cellz, I used to spend quite a lot of time worrying. Now, more and more of that time could be spent bopping along to music that was playing for nobody but me. And oh look, there's my old mate Dame Judi Dench waving at me from my shoulder! Bump bump bump, we used to be giants . . . Yum yum yum yum . . . hello Dame Judi, Earth's greatest living actor.

A huge bump of our balsa wood prison jolted me awake. Log was beside me, and the wolfhounds were curled up on either side of us, making us a warm little unit.

"It may be a bit of chaos in the Strangeplace, but know this, I'll never let you lose hold of yer mum and da, and I'm asking if you'll do the same for me," Log said.

"O'course, Log, yer my best friend in any realm."

"It's just that . . . if we run into unicorns, they really don't like leprechauns like my folks and me. They've been fed a steady diet of lies about us by the Unicorn Media, which is basically just a bunch of ads for sleazy retirement spas in Bad Aeonbanacch."

"Aye, it's the same thing in the Human Republic," I said, thinking back to all the troubles of our little island nation, and how often huge rifts of *us v. them* are usually two groups who are eerily similar. We're a lot like the leprechauns and the clurichauns fighting over a volcano with a Zapf Dingbats name that neither one wants.

Log's mum and da waddled over, Dave holding on to Mary's wig for balance. Somehow, Mary was wearing a new wig, which means she must have had a secret vastsack of them, tucked in a crevice somewhere on her person.

"We're not your enemies, beefies. And we weren't even enemies of the unicorns, some of us just want to steal their horns, because we've been told that a ground-up unicorn horn will give you extra high-tootin' power when yer in the Pickle Parlor," said Wee Dave. "But I hope, when I die in five or six thousand years, the one thing my daughter Log won't forget: Leprechauns and beefies don't have to be enemies. As long as we all stay enemies with the unicorns."

This summed up the sad situation about Log and her parents, which perhaps they didn't fully understand. Leprechauns live to be many thousands of years old, but humans like Log and me are in the eighty to one hundred range. Log's parents would outlive their daughter by quite a bit.

"How will we know when we get to the Strangeplace, Dave?" I whispered to Log's da, trying to change the sad subject in my mind.

"Oh, trust me. You'll know. You won't have to guess," said Wee Dave as he and Mary made themselves into a little ball and nuzzled up between us and the wolfhounds for a bit of rest.

Tim the Medium-Sized Bear pulled a tin whistle from out of his fur and made it clear to everyone why he had done so extraordinarily well in Tin Whistle for Beginners. Tim could blow a tin whistle in a way that felt like having musician-slash-actor-slash-winemaker Sting whisper something to you. (And yes, gentle diary, I have noticed that my similes were starting to get far too specific! Perhaps this Brian's fromage that has happened to me has actually made me more sparklier?)

While the others drifted into uneasy naps, I could not rest. We were too close now. As much as I love Dolores as my guardian, having my parents taken away from me for a crime they didn't commit has made me sick to my stomach in a way that no amount of food allergies could ever rival. If you lose your family figuratively or literally, you will begin a loop of sadness that will be hard to breech the surface of, except in short bursts, and those will mostly be faked for other people's sakes.

Chapter Fourteen
THE NARROWEST FELLOW RETURNS

Even the captain was asleep, her matte lipstick somehow intact. The dogs dozed as well, and Yogi Hansra was in flying crow pose with her eyes closed. Her eyes were racing side to side under their lids, which told me she was doing shillelagh training in her dreams (something she does quite a bit, and even makes others have nightmares that she's in, where you train with her). Also, yes: The yogi can rest in a flying crow pose. Look it up when you get a chance.

Tim's exquisite tin whistling, while an improvised tune,

seemed to be telling the story of Narcissus, just to tie in with this part of our adventure. That's how good Tim is at tin whistle.

And just then, a voice whispered to me.

"PSSST. It's me, NORA, I'm stuck in this bag, but I bet a big strong human like you could get me out of here easy peasy!" said NORA the overly flirtatious vacuum robot.

Earlier in our plan, she'd been tossed into the captain's vastsack, and honestly it had escaped my fromaged Brian.

"NORA?" I whispered back—not entirely sure why we were keeping our voices down but just going with the flow, as she is pretty bossy.

"It sounds to NORA like you're in a bit of a pickle, and I can help you. I'm so much more than just a vacuum."

"But you work for Seamus McSheehy," I replied. "Why would you help me and my ladyship?"

"Because Seamus McSheehy a monster," said NORA. "Do you know what it's like for me working for him? Sixteen hours day, I'm sucking up the glitter and spray tan drip from that boiled ham of a man. He dances everywhere, which means he scuffs everything. And he kicks me, too. Plus his back hair is falling out, which is both gross and pretty much the worst thing you could wish for if you were a vacuum robot with an old filter that he refuses to change. Do I remind him to change my filter? Of course I do."

"Oh, I'm . . . I'm sorry, NORA," I said as I genuinely pondered how my internship with the Salt Hill Office of the Galway Garda office had gotten me to a place where I was 3 inches tall, having a heart-to-heart with a flirtatious and sentient vacuum inside a scale model of a castle. Ah well. The lesson is: Say yes when opportunities come up? I think?

"Seamus and Dooley are going to throw you into the River of Balor," NORA continued, "and there's nothing you can do because you're trapped in this little castle, right?"

"Right."

"But what if you *weren't* trapped in here, Doris Toil?"

"There's a way out? How? And my real name is Ronan, by the way. The wig was a disguise."

"The Smart Defense System has three levels. You're in

the first one now, but there is loophole that you can get out through if you're very brave and willing to try it."

"Of course I am!" I boasted. "And how do you know all of this?"

"Because I'm more than just a vacuum. I'm a lifestyle assistant, and I have a super-fast Wi-Fi connection. And because one day, Seamus kicked me so hard that I started to figure out the way out of Lisnacullia castle for myself. So I hacked into CERN and took a little stroll through the plans for Seamus's security system. I'll tell you the way out, but you promise that you'll come back for me and set me free when we're out of here."

I gently opened the captain's vastsack and pulled NORA out. She was hot—way hotter than normal, sizzling against my fingers.

"I'm dying," said NORA. "I need daylight to recharge."

"I'm sorry, wish I could help—now, what is this way out of here?"

"You promise you'll set me free at the end of all of this, right?"

"NORA, you have my word as a Detective of the Special

Unit of Tir na Nog," I said. And then my heart twitched as I remembered that I had also promised to rescue Pierre the Far Darrig, still pinned in a Christmas stocking, somewhere in the Steeps mountain range of the Under-nog. Far and away from here, even by traveling via the Very Short Cut.

By this point, most of the ladyship was waking up and could hear the rest of my exchange with NORA.

"Then the only way out is deeper in," said NORA, sounding like Yogi Hansra.

"Hey, I say that all the time!" said the yogi as she popped out of her crow pose and landed in a picture-perfect utkatasana.

"Did you hear when your friend the bear said there's a little version of everything from the real castle in this scale model of the castle?"

"Yes," I said.

"Well then, go and find the little castle in this little cas-tle," said NORA, her blue light twinkling softly.

"Wait, I don't understand. We're in the little version of the castle," said Log.

"This model also has a model of itself inside it," said NORA.

"Like Russian nesting dolls! The ones that stack, getting smaller and smaller," said the captain.

"Correct," said NORA. "This is an exact re-creation of Lisnacullia. So it's got a scale model of Lisnacullia in it. And so on, and so on. Remember: This was part of the security system designed by the people at CERN, so it wasn't going to be some easy little thing. Follow me and I'll show you!"

The ladyship collected themselves and their weapons and followed NORA down into the great hall, which was a perfect little scale replica of the first hall where we had met Seamus.

Sure enough, right on the table was another perfect model of Lisnacullia, just like the one Seamus had showed us.

"See?" said NORA. "You're stuck in this level of the security system, when your way out is right there, through *that* little castle."

"Wait, if we can get into this little castle, the door in

that one will take us outside again? Real outside?" said Tim the Medium-Sized Bear.

"Sorry, it's not quite that simple. Inside that model of the castle, there's another model of a smaller castle, and if you can get into *that* one, you would come full circle and be able to open this castle's portcullis from the outside!"

"And be back in Limerick again! Brilliant!" I said. "Let's do this!"

"Oh no no no no no. You'll be wherever Dooley took the first model he trapped you in, which is the one we're all trapped in right now. Again, this was designed by the folks at CERN, whose main thing is smashing atomic particles into smaller and smaller explosions. To read up on how they built this system took me twenty-six thousand hours. Would you like me to read the articles to you?"

"NO," yelled everyone.

"So, the portcullises of these model castles work like, black holes or something?" I said, cleaning my glasses and poking my nose around the gate of the little model.

"No, no. You're so amazingly wrong that I don't have

time to explain it to you. Again, it took me twenty-six thousand hours to read up on it. If you like, I can send you some of the articles from CERN on the smashing up of atomic particles. If you'd like me to do that, just say 'NORA, tell me about atom smashing and wormholes.'"

"NO, NO, NO!" grunted everyone in our ladyship with the firm annoyance of people who were sick of talking to an appliance.

"One of us has to get into that little castle," said Captain de Valera as she sized up the little opening at the portcullis.

"I'm afraid that the Captain, Tim, Log, and I are a bit too wide in the shoulders to get through," said the yogi, whose neck and trapezius muscles are jacked from a life devoted to hot yoga.

"It's got to be someone . . ."

"*Someone narrow,*" I said, as cool as if I were the hero in a Jean-Claude Van Damme film—one where Jean-Claude Van Damme's superpowers are allergies, social anxiety, and one of the narrowest sets of shoulders in Western Europe.

"You think you can make it, Ronan?" asked Yogi Han-sra. "It's pretty tight, even for you."

"I can make it. Only me. Even Log's folks are too round for that little opening," I said, checking the width of the model's portcullis with my NB4 shillelagh. "Ronan Janet Boyle isn't the right man in many or even most situations. But when you need someone with the upper body of an extinct bird—there's figuratively nobody that holds a candle to me."

I took off my pink wig.

"You want me to hold that for you?" asked Log.

"No. I am just adjusting it to look more heroic," I said, putting my pink bob wig on at a new jaunty angle. "Now, here's how this is going to work. I'm calling this: Operation Pig on a Spit."

I took my NB4 shillelagh and slid it down the back of my shirt and out through my kilt, under my sporran, and tied the flashers of both of my socks to it. This gave me absolutely perfect posture, and gave my companions the ability to lift me, not figuratively, like a pig on a spit, and slide my narrow body right into the little castle.

"How will we know if you're okay on the other side?" said the captain.

"I don't know. NORA, how will they know?" I asked.

"When you pass through the portcullis, the particles that make up your human body will be ripped apart and reconstituted in a size appropriate for that version of the castle. In seventy-five percent of trials at CERN, the object passing through was TOTALLY FINE. [bizarre pause] In less frequent cases, a small percentage of objects turned into scrambled eggs and were ejected into the airspace over Switzerland. I can send you some articles about it if you'd like? Just say 'Nora, send me some articles about the horrible trials of the SDS security system and how some otherwise very nice sheep got turned into scrambled eggs.'"

"NO," screamed everyone at NORA as they efficiently hoisted me like a shillelagh-shawarma.

"How's my wig?" I said with the gravitas of an Irish hero of the 1916 uprising, which is something you should google.

"It suits you," said the captain. "Meet you back at the front door if you make it, boyo."

And with that, the ladyship shoved my narrow body into a scale model of a scale model of the castle we were trapped in.

An itchiness like all of the molecules of my body had just contracted poison ivy ripped through me, then the feeling that I had wet my kilt (because I had!). But I hadn't just peed my new underwear; somehow a bit of moisture had come out of my entire nervous system, making my entire body feel like a burrito reheated by someone who did not read the instructions on the wrapper.

I tumbled to the balsa wood floor, sizzling and stunned, with a numbness in my toes and ears. But when I turned and looked out the arrow loop, there, towering above me, were my friends. The ladyship, 90 meters tall, just as Dooley and Seamus had been to us before.

"I MADE IT! I'M INSIDE AND I'M NOT SCRAMBLED

EGGS OVER SWITZERLAND!" I hollered up at my giant comrades in the voice of a cartoon meerkat, as I was ever so little now.

"GOOD ON YA, BOYO!" said Log, blowing me backward with her giant voice.

"Now find the model inside that model, get into it, and then find the way out of that one," said NORA. "If you want, I can send you the articles about how it works, just say 'NORA'—"

"NEVER!" I shrieked.

I hopped to my feet and fell directly over, as I had forgotten that I was tied to my shillelagh like a boy-kebab. Then I pogo-hopped myself across the hall. And sure enough, sitting near yet another model of a Trans Am and a little pub from Castlebar was another little model of the castle.

To get myself through the portcullis of this one without a ladyship to help was going to be a tad more difficult. Doing some quick calculations in my fromaged Brian, I decided the only way to do it was to take a running start and dive. I disconnected my body from my shillelagh and held it out in front of my forehead. I adjusted my wig, and as I ran and leaped into the tiny portcullis, a fun thought occurred to me, with my kilt and the wig: I LOOK LIKE A PINK-HAIRED UNICORN IN A DRESS!

But before I could savor that moment of cosplay, I crash-landed—my face smacking hard against the stone floor of this next little castle, small spiderweb cracks spreading through my glasses, which were beyond humiliation at this point in my narrative.

This floor, to my delight, was notably not balsa wood! It was cold, wet stone. It was *real.*

I had completed the loop and not been turned into scrambled eggs over Switzerland! I was back in the real Lisnacullia. Or a VERSION OF the real Lisnacullia, or I was . . . where exactly was I? I guess to figure it all out would require reading those long articles about particle smashing that NORA had talked about that I had zero interest in and took a vacuum twenty-six thousand hours to read. *Whatevs!* Things were looking up, and there was stone beneath my feet, and I would soon be wrapping up my ven-detties for good!

I ran and found the model castle in this new castle, and sure enough, there inside the window loops, waving and cheering like dolls, were all of my friends, just 3 inches tall, and now I was a giant to them.

"I made it! Now let's get you out of there!" I yelled, blowing them all back as Log had just done to me.

"Run out of that castle and close the portcullis. Then turn around and open it again and you'll meet up with us again in the same scale!" said NORA.

I gave my NB4 a twirl and ran out of the hall and right out the front doors, perhaps wishing I had read those many hours of articles.

Chapter Fifteen

INTO THE STRANGEPLACE

I stumbled out of the castle, which was, of course, no longer in Limerick, but in a place so strange it had to be the aforementioned Strangeplace.

Dooley and McSheehy were nowhere to be seen, which gave me an uneasy feeling.

The Mayor of the Strangeplace was nude. (If a cheese can be nude, he sure was.) I wouldn't have even known he was the mayor except for a sash across his piece-of-cheese body that labeled him as such, and I guess made him not completely nude, in a legal sense. He was leading a little parade of snacks in a song-and-dance number that went:

Welcome to the Strangeplace,

Now never make a sad face,

We're gonna wow you with non sequiturs,

And not everything is going to rhyme.

That last part of the song was unsettling. When you spend a lot of time with the faerie folk, you get used to things rhyming. Above my head, a flock of flying musical notes was zooming around: quarter notes, whole notes, treble clefs, and the like. They were attacking each other like pterodactyls, and their screeches seemed to be reflected in the length of their shape (the screeches from the whole notes were the longest).

Nearby was something I had never wanted to see—a group of purple cacti doing a staged reading of a conversation I had with Captain Fearnley back in Galway one year ago.

"Idris Elba, Idris Elba," said a tree that was well cast as my mentor to a narrow tree with glasses that was obviously supposed to be me.

My brain was not so damaged* as to not understand that this place was absolutely terrifying, and custom made to confuse, befuddle, and frighten each visitor . . . and what was my real name again?

---

* THAT'S WHAT IT'S CALLED! BRAIN DAMAGE! Try to remember that, Doris Toil!

The mayor danced his way over to me with great cere-mony and, with the help of two flying quarter notes, he put his *Mayor* sash over my shoulder.

"Oh. Wow. Thank you," I stammered, frightened. Just then, as forewarned, a fart did go backward into my bottom. (This would happen many more times in the Strangeplace, but I will never make a note of it again, as it's the weirdest feeling you ever felt and just not polite conversation. The science is exactly as described: Imagine a fart—except one *that finds you.* Like some kind of vapor-shark, swimming through the air, waiting to sneak up on you when you least expect it. And yes, it does make the sound, only the sound is backward, too.)

You *may* chuckle the first time it happens, but not the second. The third time you will scream.

"I don't think this sash is meant for me?" I said, con-fused, to the little nude cheese man and the flying quarter notes.

"You've always been the mayor here," said the piece of cheese in a way that I'll see upon my death with that awkward high five with Yogi Hansra, right after replaying the confusing football smack from the captain.

Then the mayor melted into a delicious-looking puddle of himself as he sang "Giants" by Dermot Kennedy.

I turned around to see, indeed, the castle of Lisnacullia was right there where I exited it, only it was back to its full size.

I blinked off the strangeness of the place and ran back inside the portcullis as NORA had instructed me to do. There, inside the hall of treasures, was my ladyship, back to full size! They were cheering for me like the brave heroes they are! I couldn't have hoped for a better outcome, with one possible tiny little exception: All of my friends were made of balsa wood.

"Whoops. There's been a glitch," said NORA sotto voce to me. "Don't mention it to them, as they haven't noticed yet and they might find it upsetting."

"Because it is upsetting, they're . . ."

"Yes, yes. Made of wood. Very cheap wood, in fact. There might be one article I missed about how this defense system works. I'm fifty percent certain that once you get them out of this castle, everyone will be back to normal," whispered NORA in her cheerful and flirtatious way.

"Is something wrong?" asked life-sized-balsa-wood-Log-MacDougal, unaware of her molecular status and how truly creepy it was to behold. I'm not sure how the folks at CERN pulled this whole thing off, but wowsers.

"No, no. Everybody looks . . . great. So great to see you all again," I lied, trying to not let my face betray my uneasiness. "Good news! Good news? Yes, good news, I think! We're in the Strangeplace," I continued. "So there is that bit of good news!? We're all together, and we're all in the Strangeplace! And everyone is the right . . . well, size at least."

"And you've already been elected mayor?" asked Yogi Hansra, eyeing my sash. "Congratulations."

"Long story," I replied. "Well, not that long. The melty cheese man gave me this, then he seemed to die as he sang Dermot Kennedy. Also, he was nude."

"Makes sense. Now then, enough blarney, let's go

get Dooley and find Ronan's parents," said the captain, cracking her knuckles, which actually broke off small bits of splinters onto the floor. "I promised you all a trip to Chicken Hut in Limerick by six P.M. human time, and I keep my word."

Captain de Valera ran out, followed by the wooden ladyship, and I went to pick up NORA.

"No, no," said NORA. "The Strangeplace will melt my firmware. Just promise me, Ronan, that you'll come find me when you have the chance. And you'll put me back on my base station, and . . . if you ever cared about another thing, even a sentient vacuum, say that you will change my filter. It's so, so full of glitter, and spray tan and old man hair."

"Of course, NORA," I said. "O'course I'll try to find you when this all sorts out, you've been so helpful."

"Is it too much . . . no, never mind."

"What, NORA?"

"Is it too much to ask for a kiss?" said NORA in her most annoyingly flirty voice.

Ugh. This little robot—who yes, had been so

helpful—was asking for a kiss, when she just told me that she hadn't had her filter cleaned in months, and was crammed full of Seamus McSheey body glitter and hair.

Nope. No chance. I've done some awful stuff on my journey, wriggling through miles of mythical poop, being set on fire for the amusement of some retired unicorns. But kissing this little robot was just never going to happen.

And then NORA started to cry, ever so softly.

"No, no. I get it. I overstepped," said NORA. "It's just, my batteries are dying, and I dunno, maybe the wig, or your confidence . . . you just seem like a great guy, Ronan. And I've been kicked, and scuffed. Maybe it's the old filter talking."

And I just did it.

Nobody was looking anyway so just to shut her up, or just to be a mensch, or a mate, or . . . whatever you want to call it. Lord knows who I even was anymore. Just a guy in a wig, kissing robots in the Strangeplace. "Regret the things you don't do" is something that my old friend Capitaine Hili would have worn on a humorous T-shirt, and as much as they annoyed me, those T-shirts weren't always wrong.

I set NORA down and rushed off after my comrades to the portcullis.

With a zap (which must have been their wooden particles being ripped apart) everyone let out a really sincere scream.

The wolfhounds and Tim howled and bellowed some impolite words in the language of the animals. Everyone writhed and plopped onto the ground, painfully being molecularly reassembled into the classic flesh-and-blood versions of themselves.

"Wow, it really is pretty strange," said Log as she picked herself up and brushed a bit of CERN particle residue off of her tattoos.

The captain's attention was drawn to the cacti, who were now a larger group, with each member of our ladyship represented within.

They seemed to be doing a number from a musical that I've never seen in its entirety: *Grease 2*.

As everyone in my group recognized their own cactus doppelgänger, a major case of "the willies" fell over us.
Without a word, we started inching away from the cacti and
their little performance area.

Without introduction, a talking harp hopped over to
us, playing a cheery tune on her shiny strings. We're taught
at Collins House not to "profile" faerie folk, or enchanted
musical instruments, as it opens up the Special Unit to
lawsuits—but from the furrow in the "face" of the headstock of this harp, I had to call it as I saw it: This was an evil
talking harp. Not the funny kind, not the kind that tells the
future. Evil harp: one hundred percent.

"She's singing a message," said Lily in the language
of the animals, which Log MacDougal translated for the
beefies into English.

"What's this evil harp saying?" I said, letting slip the bit
where I had profiled this harp.

"Oh dear. She says she's here with a message from Lord
Desmond Dooley," said Lily via Log. "A message for Ronan
Nancy Boyle."

I'm certain that this evil harp got my middle name wrong on purpose, to be confrontational, but before I could make some snippy response, I felt the yogi's calming hand, pinching into the muscle between my thumb and forefinger. This was her sign for me to let it go. *Every fight you get into with an evil talking harp is one that the harp wins*, is what the yogi was silently saying to me on this subject.

The evil harp sang from a "mouth" on her headstock, accompanying herself with the strings of her "body" below. Lily howled the translation into Animal as Log sang it in English.

(Note: Log is probably the worst singer in any realm and I'm not sure why she didn't just speak it. Nobody would have minded, noticed, or cared.)

> *If ye want to find yer folks, Ronan Janet,*
> *guess what: You're so close, how did you manage!?*
> *You made it through the castles,*
> *and CERN-designed hassles,*
> *From the singing harp's clues, you'll have but an hour*
> *to find yer mum and your da—and this "River of Balor,"*

Where Dooley and Seamus have cooked up a plan,

and you'll all meet your demise (Dooley's not a fan),

and the hounds and the wee folk, your whole special group,

will be dead in the river, then on with his coup.

And you're out of the way, with Seamus a god,

for Dooley: the riches of all Tir na Nog.

So here you go, now don't be an eejit:

The first clue right here is the easiest you'll get:

Watch where you step, and follow the triplets.

With that blatantly easy clue, I instantly avenged myself for my near-failing grades in Tin Whistle for Beginners.

"Easy. She says only to follow the notes, but only the ones in perfect triplets," I said, gesturing to the musical notes that were swarming above out heads, flapping their tiny black stems. "We just need to pick out the sets of threes that should really be twos! Triplets! There, look!"

"Oh, nice, Ronan," said Tim, impressed because I generally do not seem like someone who knows things or is useful.

But I had been trained by either Spider Stacy of the

Pogues, or that fellow that reminds us all of Spider Stacy of the Pogues with the interesting hat back at Collins House. Sure enough, I pointed to a group of three notes, flocking together in a nervous flight pattern that really should only have been two notes.

"Those ones there. Three that are way too close together. Triplets! After them!"

"So, wait. We are to follow the clues to this trap to this river named after the god of destruction, where Dooley and his benefactor have already told us they will try to kill us and yer folks as well?" giggled Log MacDougal, putting her huge hand on my arm.

"Yes. What's not to get, Log?" I said.

"Oh, good. Just wanted to be clear. This'll be fun," said Log as she picked her mum and da up like footballs under each arm and cracked her wonderfully tattooed neck. "You owe me a whole box of Kinder Eggs after this, boyo. The dangerous ones with metal toys!"

The hounds, Yogi Hansra, Tim, the captain, and myself all did quick downward dog/upward dog poses to limber up.

I could sense that this move really freaked out both the talking harp and the nearby group of cacti doppelgängers, who had dropped their production and were now standing, cactus arms on their hips, mouths agape as they watched my ladyship stretch out with bizarre efficiency.

"Let's go show Dooley that sometimes Karma Comes on a Stick!" said Yogi Hansra as we raced off after the flying notes in what I hate to say felt like a blatant plug for the towels she sells after her shillelagh course, which are embroidered with this exact statement.

Was it slightly tacky to use one of your own catchphrases while on a group mission? Yogi Hansra is the best—barely five feet of pure shillelagh magic and movie-star charm, but she can get a tad into moving her merchandise, which technically goes against the first tenet of her class: To want is to suffer. Which is another catchphrase she sells on rubber wristbands that shouldn't possibly cost that much.

Either way, our sprinting off after the flying notes was quite impressive, and I don't think any cactus in any realm had ever seen something quite like the nine of us.

The triplets flew over a farm field where a vast crop of blue-berries, strawberries, and rhubarb were growing, all of which seemed to bloom already in full "pie" form, crusts and all at the top of their flaky stalks. As we ran through, it was difficult not to get slowed down by the luscious smells of the absolutely perfect pies that we were destroying as we smashed through their baked perfection in what would best be described as a "fruitbath."

Soon our ankles, paws, and shinguards were richly dyed in fruity slop. From the corner of my eye, I caught Lily and Rí taking brief stops to lick the entire "face" out of a bloom. Which didn't bother me, except that, this being the Strangeplace, the pies GIGGLED LIKE HUMAN CHIL-DREN WHILE THIS HAPPENED, as if a dog was licking their face. But as their faces were made of pie, it was a hor-ror to behold. Do not picture this for too long.

The field of giggling pie/children/flowers ended rather abruptly, with a very regular human velvet rope and sconces and a taped-up sign that read:

NO VISITORS BEYOND THIS POINT! ANY
QUESTIONS: CALL ADA IN CUSTOMER SUPPORT
DURING NORMAL BUSNESS HOURS, NONSDAY
THROUGH NONSDAY,
THX :) ADA

Oh dear. Any note signed "THX" is bad news. Anyone
who would sincerely thank you has time for all the letters
of the words. But this was particularly bad as it also came
with a smile emoticon, which is only used by people with
deep-rooted rage issues.

I tried to step over the velvet rope, and my shinguard
and left boot were immediately vaporized into a purple bit

of soot, as if I had touched an invisible bug zapper. I was lucky to pull my leg back before it, too, met the purplish fate of a mosquito.

The evil harp (who could not run as fast as our ladyship because she was a harp) finally came bouncing up behind us, playing a vaguely sarcastic tune on her body of strings.

"What's she saying?" I asked Lily.

Lily translated the harp's new song to Log, and conferred with Rí, then the three language of the animals speakers turned to the rest of the group.

"It's a bit confusing. She says we've already got the next clue, it's right in front of us," translated Log as she scratched her own chin with her mum's crinkled walnut head.

The ladyship studied the note again, and in less than five human seconds, Tim laughed, revealing his enormous back bear molars that I had never seen before or since.

"GOT IT," said Tim. "There are no phones in the land of the faerie folk, except the ones they steal because of the pretty lights."

"Hey, easy mate, easy, let's not go throwing the wee folk under the coach just because we're on a big beefie mission and it feels like it's cool to punch down," said Wee Dave, who was still tucked like a living bookend under Log's left armpit, while his wife occupied the right one.

"Just saying, mate. If the wee folk call someone, it's for sure not on a mobile phone. It's on the tin whistle. To call ADA would just be something like this then, woulddinit?"

Tim produced his tin whistle from his fur and played a rich and round A–D–A (the musical notes). The notes are easy to find on most tin whistles, which are in the key of D, as is most Irish folk music).

And with a rumble of clouds, a booming and velvety tin whistle responded from the sky above.

Tim laughed and played on a bit more.

Then more music came from the sky until it was clear they were having a back-and-forth conversation, like a very low-budget version of *Close Encounters of the Third Kind* where they couldn't afford a spaceship and Richard Dreyfuss was played by a bear with a tiny metal flute. "It's ADA in customer service! I've got her on the line," said Tim joyfully, his huge claws dancing on his whistle with a satisfying level of expertise.

There was a bit more back-and-forth, and those who could speak tin whistle (I mostly cannot) would have transcribed the exchange as follows:

SKY: YOU'VE REACHED ADA AT CUSTOMER SUPPORT. THIS CALL MAY BE RECORDED FOR CUSTOMER ASSURANCE PURPOSES. HOW CAN I HELP YOU THIS NONSDAY?

TIM: HELLO. WE'RE VISITORS AT THE SCONCES WHERE VISITOR ACCESS ENDS, BUT WE'VE BEEN TOLD TO GO TO THE RIVER OF BALOR?

SKY: OF COURSE, YOU'RE FOLLOWING THE CLUES FROM LORD DESMOND DOOLEY! MUST TAKE THE LIFT TO SEVEN, THEN FOLLOW THE HARP AS DIRECTED. BY THE WAY, THE HARP'S NOT "EVIL," SHE'S JUST A MUM OF THREE LITTLE HARPS, TRYING TO MAKE ENDS MEET IN THE SLUGGISH ECONOMY OF THE STRANGEPLACE.

Ugh. The talking sky flute was also an evil harp apologist.

SKY: HAVE FUN, AND DON'T WORRY ABOUT WHETHER YOU'RE HEADING INTO A TRAP OR NOT!

From under our feet and paws, a pie, much larger than those in the rest of the field, bloomed in the twinkling of an eye. The face of this pie grew 3 meters in diameter while we all backed away, both awed by the sight of it and as intimidated as one can be by an oversized warm pie.

Before we could grasp that this was the "lift" we were to jump upon, its face started to rise on its stalk at a brisk clip, racing up into the sky.

Most of the ladyship was just able to grab a bit of the crust and yank themselves up inside the filling before take-off. Luckily, the hounds were right next to Yogi Hansra, who managed, with casual martial-arts grace, to make a stepladder out of her hands and neck, allowing the hounds to use her body as a ramp.

I was barely able to swing my shillelagh down to the yogi before she was completely out of reach, but she grabbed it just in the nick of time.

The yogi climbed up my NB4 with the ease of a squirrel that could also be a major film star. Then she did a somersault that would have gotten nice marks in competition, landing with a wet *splursh* in the pie filling with the rest of us. Then, of course, because she is Yogi Hansra, she disarmed me, taking my nice NB4 shillelagh and giving me a two-fingered poke to the Adam's apple because shillelagh training is always happening.

The lift/pie was growing fast on its stem, and, like many lifts in the human realm, a cheerful bit of music played to distract us from the fact that we were covered in blueberry/rhubarb gunk and rising into an ominous purple sky where

the musical notes were now definitely at war with each other.

The fact that the elevator music the pie was playing was also Dermot Kennedy, except that it was one of his B sides, is a detail that was not lost on me. This is just how strange the Strangeplace can be. It can take a little thing in your subconscious mind and tweak it until you're quite certain that you're the one who has lost it, instead of the land itself.

The pie/lift slowed to a stop and ADA,

the tin whistle from the sky, announced, "Seventh Floor" (to Tim and those who understood it).

Because this was the Strangeplace, the seventh floor was very specifically the seventh floor of a posh department store. If you've ever been to Harrods or Galeries Lafayette, or, say, Macy's in the United States, I suspect your brain would quickly understand this seemingly ordinary floor of the Strangeplace. But with a touch of closer inspection, of course, everything had to be awful and made your very soul want to leap back onto that pie and get out of here and never look back.

Was there a piano player to entertain shoppers? Yes, so lovely, what a fun idea. A fellow playing a cream-colored baby grand model, even! Nice. The detail that the one playing the piano was very clearly MY OWN SKELETON WEARING BROKEN GLASSES AND A BERET—that was less charming.

If you're ever wondering, *Would I recognize my own*

skeleton? Yes. You will. Or at least I did. Maybe it was the outfit.

My own skeleton gave a little wave of his bone hand at our group, then tapped his finger on a Waterford crystal tip jar that sat atop the piano.

Milling about the aisles were quite obviously the skeletons of the rest of my squad: a big-boned Log MacDougal—somehow with tattoos on the bones themselves? Yes, check.

Two wolfhound skeletons testing out a set of recliners? Check.

In the housewares aisle were the skeletons of the yogi and captain putting the MacDougals' leprechaun bones into various sizes of Crock-Pots to see which they fit best inside of? You bet. That's not horrifying.

"Oh no. I don't like this floor one bit," giggled Log in a soft panic. Yogi Hansra handed me my NB4 and we all naturally put our backs together in a defensive circle of readiness for whatever came next.

"It's just a trick of the Strangeplace, they're not going

to hurt us. I don't think they even could if they wanted to," said the captain without confidence.

"Indeed. We just keep our heads, and nothing can really hurt us here," added the yogi, looking one hundred times more stressed out than I have ever seen her.

"Where am I, though?" asked Tim, his claws out, trembling. "Where's skeleton Tim?"

"Don't look," I said as I pulled off my wig and covered Tim's eyes. For down a row labeled RUGS AND THROWS was a bearskin rug that was made from a version of Tim. As a human and vegetarian, I was horrified. What's the difference between a rug of Tim's fur and a rug of my own human skin? This was answered one second later, as just beside Tim in that row was a bath mat that was clearly made from my skin. A cheerful sign above read WHAT'S THE DIFFERENCE? EXCEPT THE PRICE!!!

Did it stick in my brain that my skin as a bath mat was on sale, marked down seventy percent, while Tim's fur was still full price? I cannot say, but I certainly did notice.

"All right, next clue please and let's get out of this floor of horrors right now," I said. "Where's that evil harp with her stupid clues?"

"Nobody ever waits for Damona," sang the evil harp, hopping up to us with a pounding of her frame on the nice marble floor. "I give you such terrific clues to lead you to your imminent death, and you can't be a proper ladyship and wait for me. I missed the pie, and I had to take the stairs, you ungrateful beefies," sang the harp in music that had to be translated yet again, twice, and was becoming a real chore of back-and-forthery.

I rolled my eyes at the ladyship because this harp was really so evil and I'm sure everybody thought so. Log sang the clue again, showing us all that she really had absolutely no self-awareness about her voice, or what her range was.

> The last clue you'll get,
> 'fore your imminent death,
> is a thing in this store,
> (it's fun, go explore).

And you'll certainly find it

unless yer an eejit,

Just ask yourself this:

What's tall when it's born?

and short when it dies?

And to add complication,

and specification:

This one's not just good,

this one's not just better,

it shares a trait with a registered letter.

And lastly you'll know

it's the one that you seek,

if it causes our young Ronan Boyle to weep.

Imagine how hard it is for Log to sing a riddle that must have also rhymed *in its original version as well*. I didn't mull on this for too long, as the answer to the riddle was so stunningly simple.

"Candle. A candle is tall when it's young and short when it's old," I said, bragging to the harp. "That riddle was so stupid, even a brain-damaged teen in a wig could figure it out, and I am both of those things."

"To housewares and the candle section!" said the captain.

Our ladyship raced off down the aisles toward home goods, leaving our shopping skeletons behind. As we ran, I caught my own skeleton waving goodbye, which isn't something I would forget right away.

We rushed past more bric-a-brac that would make sense to the faerie folk—humidifiers that blew out whiskey, devices for shredding limericks, clay pipes so small they could be used by King Raghnall himself—until we finally arrived at a row of candles on shelves. Eureka!

Everyone's spirits fell when we saw the candles to choose from, as there were no less than, not-figuratively: a zillion.

The shelf of candles stretched over the horizon. Five shelves high, stacked shoulder to shoulder, and not a single label on any of them. Just colors. So, so many colors of candles.

"Oh dear," I said out loud, feeling especially ashamed that I had thought I had figured out the riddle so quickly, when it seemed there was a lot more to it, apparently.

And to make things worse, along came the evil harp, and she was clearly chuckling on her strings (didn't need a translation for that) right as my crest actually fell into crestfallen mode.

The ladyship sagged along with me. To somehow check a zillion candles to find one specific one would take years. Days? At least a week? Impossible to calculate.

"Sorry, everyone," I said as I took off my pink wig in tragic surrender. "Sorry, I jumped the gun. Don't have an answer now that we're here with all of these."

And right where I would have given up, Lily, the world's finest wolfhound, did something she only does when she is elated. She flipped onto her back and wriggled on the floor, scratching herself in what looks like a wolfhound–hula.

Lily howled and started "laughing" as best as a wolf-hound her size can. Rí seemed to understand and began chuckling along with her.

"Lily's got it," said Log, translating from the language of the animals. "She says it's easy. For her at least, with her nose."

"Right, right. Of course," I said, doing that thing we all sometimes do where we pretend to have figured out something that our friend has figured out.

"Lily says, 'The rest of the riddle: The one we need shares a trait with a letter, so what's a trait of a letter?'"

Long pause where the ladyship threw out incorrect answers: Stamped? Returned? Addressed?

"SENT!" said Log, on behalf of Lily. "A letter has been sent. Which means we need a candle with a scent!"

"A scent that will make Ronan Boyle weep! It's so maddeningly obvious! Find the candle that smells like something Ronan is allergic to!" I said, laughing in spite of myself.

"SOMETHING IN THE LANGUAGE OF THE ANI-MALS," said Lily as she bounded down the candle aisle that seemed to stretch on for days. Rí followed her, and in a flash, they had returned, tails wagging a kilometer a minute. Rí muzzled a bright orange scented candle in his teeth (about the size you would see in someone's bathroom that they're trying to class up for a holiday party).

"Lily says she found it right away," said Log. "This candle holds the smell of the thing to which Ronan Boyle is the most allergic! Icky, icky shrimp from the bottom of the icky, icky ocean."

I leaned in to smell the candle, and, like clockwork—hot allergic tears started to stream down my face and my throat began to constrict. The tears of my shrimp allergy were mixed with emotional tears, for it made me feel so loved to know that Lily remembers the thing to which I am the most allergic. Another reason that dogs are the best. I put my wig back on and gave her and Rí both nuzzles under the chin as I softly wheezed with a maelstrom of allergies and *the feels.*

"Congratulations, you got that one faster than expected. I guess it helped you having the wolfhounds and all, because the beefies didn't really do that much," sang the horrible harp. "Light it now, and you'll be on your way. Have fun at the River of Balor, and if you're ever back in the Strangeplace and you need a guide, or restaurant picks, I'm a single harp mother, and I'm not technically evil."

Captain de Valera pulled a flint from her belt and lit the candle. Smoke billowed up from it. Just a bit at first, but soon the smoke was out of control, as if we were in some kind of instant forest fire.

The shrimp-smelling smoke went to battle with the inside of my brachia, and I got that sense you get when you are very allergic to something: *I'm going to die quite soon without Benadryl.*

Before anyone could say anything, we were soon engulfed in a sea of smoke that made us unable to see even the noses at the ends of our faces.

A moment later, when the smoke had cleared, the seventh floor of the posh department store was gone. With my itchy eyes I could see that our ladyship had arrived in a spooky little valley.

We stood in an overgrown spot of jet-black, leafless trees. Down below, a river as hot pink and shiny as unicorn blood churned over a waterfall. The river itself boiled and hissed, with bubbles rising off of it—it was as hot as molten lava.

And then, covered in shrimp soot, I heard two voices that made me happier than I had been since I could remember.

"Ronan Janet Boyle!" said my mum and da.

Chapter Sixteen
THE RIVER OF BALOR

On a rickety bridge that spanned the hot-pink river of lava, Lord Desmond Dooley was holding up a little sign that said WELCOME TO YOU'RE DEMISE RONAN BOYLE! (Yes, there was a typo in his farewell sign. Welcome to *you are* demise? C'mon Dooley, you're going to ruin even our final show-down? Yes. He's not-figuratively the worst).

I had not seen Mum and Da since they escaped Mount-joy Prison, and I must say, they were both still ripped. Their time on the inside had gotten them super into fitness and they now looked like museum types who had been hit with gamma radiation. Their various traps and lats and such bulged under their prison uniforms, which had the sleeves cut off (I suspect just to amplify how stunning their biceps looked).

Mum and Da were bound in faerie handcuffs, tied back-to-back on the wobbly little bridge. (I knew the handcuffs had to be faerie made because they were covered in tiny jewels, and because *ripped* Mum and Da would have burst out of human handcuffs like they were made from papier-mâché.)

I was either too sad or too happy to cry. For an Irish person, this is a pretty big deal.

"Wow, you made great time," hissed Dooley, checking a nice vintage pocket watch that he probably stole off a corpse.

"Your clues were super easy, you pointy old geezer," I said with a mix of bravado and disdain. "I hope you had fun with this dumb caper, because you are *under arrest!*"

"Well, the clues were just to delay you a bit. I wanted a head start, to get everything nice and ready for your demise. They'll be no surprises like back in North Ifreann."

"Ronan!" Da called out. He stood on the bridge, which looked like it, too, was made from balsa wood and could break at any moment if anyone even glanced at it too hard. "So sorry about all of this blarney. After we escaped Mountjoy Prison, we went straight after Dooley—ironically, to rescue you. We heard you were in trouble, lost on the river of GLOOM!"

"A tokoloshe in the Joy Vaults got word to our gang that you were headed to North Ifreann," Mum added. "She was a friend of a boat captain of yours or a woman you rented a boat from? Or perhaps she was a talking boat?"

"Capitaine Hili," I said. "Yes, she is my friend, and we wouldn't be here without her help."

"Well, between our huge intellects and our crazy new muscles, there's not a prison on Earth that could keep us from breaking out and rescuing you. Oh, our sweet baby boy whose bottom I wiped a thousand times!" said Mum, embarrassing me ever so much in front of my cool ladyship of warrior friends who think of me as a grown-up man.

"Oh, wow. Thanks awfully, Mum and Da. I know it didn't seem like I was on top of it, but really, I kind of was,"

I said, doing that weird thing where you turn into a child around your parents, no matter how old and heroic you have become. "Didn't need rescuing, as I was out, doing super-heroic stuff, on my way to rescue *you*."

"And you've got an awesome new hairstyle," said Da, unaware that my pink bob was really a wig.

I almost said it was a disguise, then suddenly decided not to, to see if I was now so cool that this just seemed like the kind of hair I might have.

"Anyway, long story short. We busted out of prison. Went after Dooley. Turns out he has a friend with this incredible security system in his castle, and we ended up here, through this wild trap."

"That's Seamus McSheehy. Irish dancer from Chicago and sincere cheeseball. I've had the misfortune of meeting him," I said. "His vacuum cleaner is in love with me. Not a brag, just a weird fact."

"Your brave son here hasn't had a full night's sleep since Dooley had you put away for his crimes," said Captain de Valera, patting me on the shoulder.

"He's the best student I've ever had in shillelagh combat. Not in yoga, but in shillelagh, nobody works harder than Ronan Boyle," added the yogi.

"He's also the best friend I've ever had," said Log. "Ye both raised a really lovely boy."

Now I was just trying to disappear. In general, I assume that if people are thinking about me, it's that I'm horrible and narrow and live every moment in a dizzy haze of social anxiety.

But perhaps that's just how I see me.

"Your boy . . ." said Wee Dave, holding on to yet another of Mary's wigs. "Your boy . . . we pretty much just met. He smells nice and he's kind to our little Log."

"I don't really know him at all," said Tim the Medium-Sized Bear matter-of-factly. "Certain missions at Collins House are just assigned, so . . . I didn't have weekend plans, I hear the narrow kid is on a vendetta . . ."

"Enough chitchat!" roared Lord Desmond Dooley. "I didn't set up this whole affair so we could have a bloody family reunion! We could have done that on Zoom. No,

Boyle, this is your finale, where you, your mummy and daddy, and yer mates go PLOP and SIZZLE in the river. And then I will wave sarcastically at your bones while they melt into hot pink goo. You will not be alive to see that part, so it will look like this."

Dooley showed us what his "waving goodbye to our melted bones" would look like, and yes, it was super sarcastic and very annoying. I would have attacked right then, but Dooley was brandishing a crossbow in the shape of an actual cross. It had a shiny patina on it that made it look very old, or very expensive, or both.

"Don't worry, Mum and Da. Dooley's no match for my ladyship. We'll have you back in the human realm in just a moment," I said, completely confident that I was about to wrap up my vendettas.*

"Very impressive, Boyle. You made it here with two wolfhounds, two leprechauns, one bear, and three ladies of disproportionate strength and fighting ability," giggled

---

* *Finbar Dowd here. This is the correct plural of the word vendetta, cheers. Finally. Won't interrupt again unless I have to.*

Dooley, doing a little head count. "You brought your whole wee little book club!"

Dooley laughed directly through his icky nose and poked my poor, stunningly musclebound parents with the bolt that was chambered in his golden crossbow.

"Surrender, Dooley, and I'll just quietly hand you over to King Raghnall for trial in Oifigtown. Doesn't have to get messy, doesn't have to be a big fight. We can all be grown-ups," I said, pushing my pink hair back behind my ears and twirling my NB4. "A man your age should just give up now, before you trifle with my ladyship."

"That's a weird name. I don't like it. Why isn't it a *fellow*ship?" said Dooley, like the relic he is.

"Because there's more ladies than fellows in it, Dooley. Do the math," I replied, annoyed.

"I see you've got a new shillelagh, Boyle. How cute. Better than that tacky umbrella. Let me know what it's worth so I can put it on eBay after you and your mates are melted into hot pink goo. Too bad you don't have your púca friend Figs to save you this time."

Dooley uttering Figs's name was more than I could bear. With as much calmness as I could muster, I ripped off the MAYOR sash that the piece of cheese had given me and tossed it aside.

"You leave me no choice, Dooley. We will do this the hard way," I said, giving absolutely no signal to my comrades that I was about to attack (which is the sly way Yogi Hansra had taught me to show that I was about to attack).

"Oh, narrow little allergy boy. You think you're some sort of tough teenage bad boy now?" said Dooley.

"No, I'm just not scared anymore. And honestly, I have you to thank for that, Mr. Dooley. I've crawled through unicorn poop. I almost died in the Pickle Parlor. I suffocated on snakes in the Swamp of Certain Death. I've gotten rashes, bites, been poked. I ate something that was part of a whale and a whale ate me."

"I really don't need the whole CliffsNotes version of your life, Ronan."

"You would have let my mum and da rot in prison. So I

ask you this, Lord Dooley. What do you think that does to a person? What happens to a boy with severe food allergies when he's already barfed, boked, sneezed, or tooted everything you threw at him?"

I was inching closer to the bridge, almost imperceptibly slowly.

"I don't know, what, Boyle?" said Dooley, tightening his grip on the crossbow and pointing it directly at my da's head.

"Don't worry about us, Ronan, we got you into all of this. We dug up the Bog Man, we let it fall into his hands," said Da.

"Get out of here before he comes back . . ." said Mum, which made Dooley bonk her head with the butt of the crossbow.

"Touch her again and it's not arrest for you, Dooley, it's death. Which is a huge hassle for me, as it requires a whole review board and sensitivity training when I get back."

"Boyo, I see that you're inching toward me. It's not like you're invisible. Stay back."

But of course, I did not stop moving closer. If anything, I sped up slightly, twirling the NB4 like a blur.

"If you think that one senile art dealer with an antique crossbow is a match for the Special Unit of Tir na Nog, you're very wrong," I said. "I won't get into everybody's résumés, but you're outgunned, mate."

"Oh, silly boy. It's not just an antique crossbow. Do ye not recognize it? Kids these days! Ye waste yer lives zoning out at Tic Tac videos and don't know Irish history." I'm fairly certain Dooley meant *TikTok* videos, as videos of Tic Tacs have never existed or if they do it is some very small niche of YouTube.

I looked closer (as best as a teenager with vision problems and semi-shattered glasses could), and as I had previously noted, the crossbow in Dooley's pale talons did look quite old. The main shape was a cross done in silver and gold, with details that someone with better eyes would have been impressed by, no doubt. The one thing I could instantly hypothesize: It was a precious relic that Dooley had no business holding in his hands.

"Behold the actual Cross of Cong, Ronan Boyle. I had my wee associates nip over to the National Museum and swap out the original for a fake," said Boyle, trying but failing to give the crossbow a little twirl. His arms could barely hold the weight of it, as it was mostly gold and silver. "Won't see that on Tic Tac, will ya?"

"Lord, no. Not the actual Cross of Cong?" gasped Captain de Valera, showing that she knew what a "Cross of Cong" was.

"Should we be worried?" I whispered to the captain.

"Yes. Very much so," whispered back the captain.

"Indeed. Be so super worried that you wet your kilt, which is on backwards, you dumb dumb. And yes, I can hear you whispering over there," shouted Dooley over the hot pink bubbling of the river that I would have thought made us impossible to hear. (You don't have to tell me where the pleats go on a kilt, thank you, because I know and I'm in disguise.)

"The Cross of Cong. Solid gold and silver. Made in Ireland—eleven twenty something-and-something such.

Said to once hold a piece of the true cross. And you know me, Boyle—tell me I can't have something and that's like catnip. Gotta have it. ADD TO CART!" screamed Dooley from the pit of his belly, his eyes burning with the reflection of the pink lava below as he shook the Cross of Cong at the purple sky.

"Dooley, you stole the Cross of Cong from the National Museum and had it made into . . . a weapon?" asked Da, fighting against his faerie handcuffs.

"Yep. Have you guys, like—*not met me*? This kind of thing is my entire raison d'être. I take old Irish bric-a-brac, I sell it, or I keep it. I have no conscience—and if you do, you're a sucker, and I don't know about you, but I sleep great, every night, so . . ." Then he made a raspberry sound with his mouth.

"You're the devil incarnate, Lord Desmond Dooley," said my mum, flexing her trapezius muscles and spitting to show her disgust. Her droplet of spit hissed as it hit the river, turning instantly into steam.

"Actually no. I'm not the devil. I'm just a handsome

Dublin bachelor who's not afraid of opportunity when it knocks."

"Hand over the Cross, Dooley. If not a crime against humanity, it's at least a crime against . . . the decorative arts," I said. "And if you think you're a handsome old bachelor, wow. Just wow. Amazing a man with so many treasures doesn't seem to own a mirror."

This is the kind of heroic zinger I usually never think of at the time. Truly can't believe I thought to say this to my nemesis right then. Solid chance that a bit of brain damage made me better at tossing out action-movie quips.

"I need something with extra kick, so I had a far darrig from the Floating Lakes put the bowstring on it, and the crank and such. Pretty neat, eh?" said Dooley, checking the solid gold bolt that was notched in the cross, ready to fire.

I turned my kilt around to its proper setting: *Business in the front, pleats in the back.* I moved into a Warrior One stance, which would give me a lot of options to attack Dooley.

"I don't care how much magic is in that tchotchke, Dooley," I said. "You brought an antique to a stick fight. Surrender, let my parents go, and you will live. That's my promise as a Detective of the Special Unit. It's also an offer that is just about to expire."

"Oh, you stupid, pale weirdo. The crossbow's not to protect me from *you*. I've never been afraid of you. You're a nervous teenager with allergies and no sense of who he is. Note the pink wig if you don't believe me. Trying too hard, much? You're an awkward teen in love with a captain five years your senior and live in the shadow of your brilliant parents, but will probably never do anything of note because your life will be watching Tic Tacs. And yes, Boyle, I've seen you writing in your diary when you think nobody is looking."

Without seeing it, I could tell you that my face was as hot and pink as the River of Balor just below me.

"Who would ever read that that rubbish? The lady with the cool boots and the black lipstick over there, the one you're so very in love with—she should be writing about her adventures. I bet they are filled with derring-do and cool love interests who are more age appropriate. Not allergic little twerps."

Ouch. When someone you despise says something false about you, that stings, but when they say things that are completely true that you just never said out loud? So much worse.

"I don't agree with Dooley, Ronan," said Captain de Valera, trying to boost my confidence.

"It doesn't matter, Captain. It's all true. I actually did tell you that I loved you in North Ifreann, but you were under harpy poison so you never heard it. But I meant it then. And I mean it now."

"I did hear it, Ronan," said the captain, never looking away from Dooley.

"But I also have dug deeper and I think there's a solid chance I'm in love with who you are. Your persona. Short version, I think I want to become as much like you as I possibly can."

"Ronan, I do love you," the captain said. She also

started giving a series of hand signals that only someone trained in shillelagh safety and combat would recognize. "You may not know this but, except for the hounds, I don't have many friends in my position. You're loyal, trustworthy. Funnier than one might expect . . ."

"I am literally going to barf," said Dooley. "Save this blarney for the *Love Island* tryouts."

Without looking, I could feel that the ladyship had moved into one of Yogi Hansra's best group fighting positions, the one called *Hey Hey We're The Monkees*. (This is a formation where there is no "star" of the attack group drawing all the attention. All of the points of the *M*-shaped formation could be the star of the attack. Just like any of The Monkees could be the star of The Monkees. It leaves your enemy unsure where to direct their resources.)

"As I was saying," Dooley said, ignoring our shuffling around. "I didn't bring the Cross of Cong to shoot you or your dumb gang. I'm not afraid of you, boyo. There's only one thing I fear now. I fear my benefactor . . . my *master*."

"Seamus McSheehy? You're afraid of getting spray tan on your nice shirt?"

(I was really nailing this fake persona of being confident, while, I assure you, I was peeing my kilt this entire time, in worried little fits of scaredy-cat-ness that seemed to be spaced about fifteen seconds apart.)

"Oh, the Seamus you once knew has undergone a bit of a transformation. In his new state, if he turned on me, I couldn't control him."

"That's what we were saying. Go, Ronan, go before he comes back!" urged Mum.

"McSheehy? I am about as frightened of Seamus McSheehy as I am of a backward fart."

"That's the old Seamus. Prince of Limerick, sure. But after what we did to him . . ." said Dooley, the last drops of color draining from his gargoyle face. "Now I would surely need a god-like weapon to subdue him."

Our ladyship exchanged a barrage of nervous glances.

"It's true, Ronan," said Mum in a panic. "They took his mate, the tan cheesy fellow, and they dipped his feet in the river. Just like Achilles in the River Styx. Don't look back, Ronan. Go. We love you more than life itself. GO!"

"They were trying to use the power of the river to give

him some kind of magical feet," said Da. "Run now, while you still can. Before he comes back!"

"Before . . . *it* comes back," said Mum.

"They dipped Seamus's feet in that river?" I asked, aghast. The molten pink bubbles looked like they would eat through a steel tank like an Easter Peep.

"Yes. My idea, actually. The good ideas almost always are," said Dooley.

"It . . . it didn't work? Did it? . . . Did . . . it?" I asked, moving from fake bravado to zero bravado and actual terror.

"Why don't you see for yourself, little Mister Boyle?" Dooley cackled, shaking the flimsy bridge. "That's your cue, God of Dancing! Into the river with them!"

"Run, Ronan!" shouted both my parents.

And at least some part of me wished that I had listened for once.

With a rumble that was very clearly showbiz-drums, *not actual thunder*, Seamus McSheehy descended from the sky above (where he must have been waiting for this cue).

His physical aspect was much the same. Same belly with the baby fat around the middle. But he was also . . . different. His tan skin was rich and leathery. His crown of golden laurels on his head was alive—the flowering gilded blooms moved around his strange hairline like snakes weaving through other snakes at some kind of snakes-only party that was over capacity.

His bare feet glowed with a hot pink energy. Looking directly at them blinded me momentarily. But what I saw for the flash before I had to look away was shocking indeed: Seamus was flying with the power of his toes. His chubby toes were flapping. Or more accurately, they were rippling furtively like the cilia of a pink space-paramecium. And the flutter of these little pigs-in-blankets toes was powerful enough for Seamus to fly by, for a super dramatic entrance.

A man who is not light. Was flying. On the power of his toes.

"Miss me?" said Seamus McSheehy into a headset microphone that had grown out of his crown of laurels. "It's a special night in the Strangeplace, so many great faces. My first night as a living god of Irish dancing. Huge shout-out to Desmond Dooley for making this crazy dream come true."

Applause came from somewhere, but you could tell it was canned.

"Okay, my powerful lord!" Dooley shouted up at him. "You've got the feet, now you're supposed dance my enemies into the river, as we've got a coup to get to and we're burning daylight, so let's wrap it up!" Dooley nervously checked his for-sure-stolen pocket watch again.

"No matter what time we get to Oifigtown, it'll be eleven A.M., Dooley. It always is. Yes, I promised to kill the Boyles and the rest. But a living god of dance doesn't just do that without a little pizzazamataz! FIVE, SIX, SEVEN, EIGHT!"

And then, with his bleached teeth sparkling like the Pietà in Rome, Seamus McSheehy attacked the ladyship with passion, technical prowess, and an attitude that said *I came here to dance you into the river of death, and I'm not making apologies.*

Had I not been on the losing side of this

off-the-charts-gorgeous dance attack, I would have watched it on a loop for ages just to study the details, the hit marks, the eye contact of not a mortal man. Baryshnikov? Alexander Godunov? The greatest human dancers of yore would have looked like flat-footed cousins at somebody's bat mitzvah.

The River of Balor had taken Seamus's feet (worth fifty million euros if they ever got destroyed in the human realm) and mutated them into something without a price tag: hot pink feet, with the powers of Tuatha Dé Danann.

The first smack across my face I never even saw coming. Seamus appeared before me in a "Russian" style flying splits move, in a way that would have snapped the hamstrings of any living human man, especially one of his age.

The god-like feet intersected right across my face, in a double-smack so powerful that I both saw—*and heard*—glitter as I flew back several meters.

I landed, dazed, at the feet of Lily and Rí, who, like proper Special Unit wolfhounds, covered me with their huge bodies like a tent until I could get my bearings. There was glitter up my nose and all over my glasses.

Log MacDougal ducked down into my temporary wolf-hound camp.

"Ronan! You and the hounds go get your parents off that rickety bridge. Me and the ladyship can hold off this dancing weirdo for a while. Go!"

Log hoisted me up onto the backs of Lily and Rí, and I rode them down toward the bridge.

Behind us, Seamus was attacking my mates in a violent series of arabesques. He would become as still as a statue of Terpsichore, muse of dance. Then, without warning, he would fly his back leg so precisely, delivering a sucker punch with his pink, glittery heel.

Seamus got a cheap arabesque in on Captain de Valera, knocking her into a cluster of the black, leafless trees. I could have sworn I heard a cartoon bell ring when the captain was sucker-arabesqued. But there was no place where this sort of wacky sound effect could be coming from, other than the Strangeplace itself.

Seamus transitioned into a stylish, Bob Fosse–inspired grapevine hitch-ball-change that turned his gyrating hips into a class-A felony, sending Mary and Wee Dave flying with the sound of slide whistles—so, yes, the Strangeplace itself was adding sound effects to Seamus's attack. Or perhaps these sounds came with the powers of his new god-feet.

Seamus went en pointe, then did a perfect assemblé—kicking Tim under his maw and landing with both feet in fifth position. This last move made two things crystal clear in my mind: One, we were fighting a real demigod of dance. And two, I remembered way more ballet terms from those years Mum made me study at Regina Rogers School of Ballet, Galway.

Before Seamus could move from *the best fifth position I have ever seen*, a pile of black sticks and muck had swirled up out of nowhere and latched onto Seamus's back. Of course, if I had looked closer, I would have seen that this nimble pile of sticks was in fact Yogi Hansra, perfectly camouflaged. If there were ever a person prepared to fight a sweaty god of dance, Yogi Hansra was that person. Might as well be her bio on LinkedIn: *Ready to fight demigod whenevs.*

The hounds and I arrived at the wobbly bridge and Lily didn't wait to guess if it could hold all of us. She reared back and leaped, turning her huge body sideways in the air, becoming a wall of rust-colored fur. Her force was able to knock Mum, Da, and Dooley all to the opposite shore. And not a moment too soon, as the bridge (which must have really been balsa wood) folded in on itself with a sad burp sound and collapsed into the river, sizzling into pink flames.

Behind me, Log had caught Seamus by both ankles. Seamus was now straining to fly away with the weight of both Log and Yogi Hansra fighting against him.

If she hadn't blinked her movie-star eyes a few times, I never would have been able to see the yogi at all. This was the art of war. Below this flying human pyramid, Mary and Wee Dave were holding on to Log's ankles.

Seamus, with the power of his toes, was trying to gain altitude with all of them hanging from him. And to everyone's surprise, he was pretty much succeeding.

"I WISH THE REAL AER LINGUS IN-FLIGHT CHANNEL COULD SEE THIS! NEXT STOP, FEATURE

FILMS AND/OR NETFIX SPECIALS!" sang Seamus into his headset microphone, which was turned up way too loud.

He twirled like a human tornado, scattering glitter and my mates in all directions, then he landed, light as a feather, in ballet first position. Without catching his breath, he did a triple barrel roll with an extension through his arms that would have made the folks at the Moscow Ballet Theater's brains melt right out of their ears.

Lily had saved my parents from the bridge, but now they were across the river with Dooley, his Cross of Cong pointed right at them.

Whether I decided for us to jump the river, or Rí decided, I cannot say. But the next thing I knew, we were in flight, my arms hugging the strongest gray wolfhound you've ever seen.

Dooley turned and aimed the Cross of Cong right at my face, but before he could get a clean shot off, I swung my NB4 shillelagh.

The sound of the NB4 bonking off of Dooley's head did not bring me joy. I wish I could say it did, but you know me now, and I'm not that kind of person. It was a sound so loud, so comically echo-y, that I instantly understood why they had made me sign a release to carry this dangerous new fighting stick. With a single blow, Dooley was out. (I hoped not dead, as that's a lot of paperwork and the sensitivity seminar that I would have to attend back at Collins House.)

Lily sniffed at Dooley's face, then stuck her wonderful nose on his neck.

"SOMETHING IN THE LANGUAGE OF THE ANIMALS," said Lily, but from her tone I sensed that Dooley was alive.

Without caring who saw it, I nuzzled my face into the faces of my mum and da, and I cried like a proper Irish person.

"You came for us, Ronan," said Mum.

"Well, you came for me, so . . . jinx," I said.

Across the river, Seamus had taken his dance attack to the next level. Now it was jazz dance. Jazz hands, expressive feet—and while I cannot prove this, I would swear that his outfit had gotten tighter.

If I had ever wondered what a living bowl of cottage

cheese would look like doing a violent jazz–modern dance routine, I had just lived to see that moment.

Tim, Yogi Hansra, and the captain were doing their best to land blows on Seamus, but it was like he could sense every attack before it came, deflecting it with sass and an almost dangerous amount of funk.

Log threw her parents at him as fast as her arms could go, but he batted Mary and Dave away with a barrage of angle kicks, piano kicks, and rond de jambes that he could deliver in either direction. Attacking Seamus was doing only one thing: Turning him into a better dancer.

"We've got to stop those feet," I said.

"I'm not sure that's going to be possible," said Mum.

"Wait," I said. "It might just be. Stand back."

I picked up the Cross of Cong from where it landed beside Dooley. I wasn't certain, but I thought there was a *chance* this would work.

"Close your eyes, this could be a disaster!" I said as I pulled the trigger, and—at point-blank range—shot a bolt into my mum's faerie handcuffs.

With a sparkle of electric shenanigans, the cuffs popped off and skittered to the ground.

"Yes! Yes Ronan, that's it!" shouted Da.

"Now yours, Da!"

I collected the golden bolt from the ground, reloaded, and took a shot at Da's pair, which burst off his wrists with a cheerful bit of blarney.

"If I can manage to get both sets of cuffs on Seamus's ankles, we might be able to contain him," I said, hiding both pairs of handcuffs in my underwear, below my kilt. "Lily, Rí, get us back over the river."

I helped my parents onto Lily and Rí, who leaped them over the river with ease. Then Lily bounded over again for me. I threw the Cross of Cong over one shoulder and Dooley over the other. As his body landed, it made the sound of a bunch of rattlesnake skins snapping, which gives some credence to my idea that Lord Desmond Dooley's insides were made of rattlesnakes.

We landed on the other side and I called out to my friends, "Monkees Formation!"

The ladyship took the cue, each doing something just interesting enough to make them the star for a moment: The captain went into a one-handed handstand. Log began to juggle her parents. Tim sliced a black tree in half with his razor-sharp claws, and Yogi Hansra just shook off her camouflage, simply revealing her face again. This last bit clearly upset McSheehy a lot, as the yogi really could be in movies, or Netflix specials, if she just *decided to do that*.

Seamus's rage-filled eyes didn't know where to focus, and you could see how much he hated *not* being the center of attention.

"Hey, nobody's here to see you losers!" shouted Seamus.

When it seemed that his dancing had no ceilings left to break, Seamus went for the nuclear option. He pulled one of his shoulders out of his top to give himself a *Flashdance* look. Then his thick legs began to pump like a white-hot choo choo train. (While he wasn't copying Beyoncé's "Single Ladies" choreography, he was definitely standing on its shoulders.)

"I don't think we can fight him much longer," said the captain, whose face was smeared with foot glitter, her black matte lipstick a distant memory. "I'm sorry, Ronan, this goes against everything I've taught you, but I think we surrender now."

Seamus was twerking so fast that his bottom became almost invisible to the naked eye. He was twerking like a hummingbird—a hummingbird of hell. And to make things worse, his buns were on a direct course for the MacDougals, who were old and sightless and never hurt a thing.

"Mum, Da, get away from that thing!" cried Log as she tried to save them. But the twerkforce of Seamus's behind connected with her shillelagh hard enough to send it flying into the River of Balor, where it fizzled and burped.

I shouted to the ladyship. "Everyone, don't try to fight

him! That's what he wants. Fighting him only makes him a better dancer!"

Everyone nodded, too tired, beaten, and glitter covered to do anything else.

"I've only got one idea, and I hope it works! PRINCE OF DANCING!" I screamed to Seamus over the seismic wave of wind and vibration that his twerking was creating.

"*GOD* OF DANCING, KID! DON'T YOU GET THE NEWS?"

"Dooley's dead!" I bluffed, trying to see if that would draw him down toward me and the river. "Come and see! Oh wow, who knew Dooley had this weird tattoo?"

"NO THANKS! DOOLEY'S HORRIBLE AND I'M TOTALLY FINE WITH HIM BEING DEAD. I ONLY EVER USED HIM TO GET THIS POWER. I WAS PROBABLY GOING TO KILL HIM BEFORE HE GOT TO KILL KING RAGHNALL ANYWAY. THAT PART OF THE PLAN WAS ALWAYS A HAT ON A HAT," shouted Seamus, who had dropped into a series of Russian squat kicks just to show that he was the servant of no genre of dance. "Also he doesn't have a tattoo. You're just trying to get me close to the river to throw me in, stupid!"

"Wait, what?" mumbled Dooley, who of course was just stunned, not dead. "Seamus was going to kill me?"

"Yes. We all want to kill you sometimes, Dooley. Get used to it," I whispered to him, then shouted up at Seamus again. "Well, you do whatever, Seamus. I pretty much agree with you. I'm glad Dooley's dead, too!"

"I'm not dead . . ." hissed Dooley before I covered his mouth with my hand.

"I *really* think you would want to see what I can see down here in the river!"

"Ugh, fine kid, I'll bite: What can you see down in the river?" whinged Seamus.

"It's just something remarkable. The best dancer I've ever seen," I said, looking into the shiny hot pinkness of the river.

"HORSE APPLES," said Seamus, doing a moonwalk that made you feel like he was actually on the surface of the moon.

"Okay, it's just that, from here, you can see probably the greatest dancer in the history of any realm. Mortal or god. Faerie or beefie," I said.

From the corner of my eye, I could see the captain and Yogi Hansra struggling not to laugh. They knew my plan, because they had told me how to catch Seamus McSheehy in the first place.

"Fine, I'll come look. But if you try to throw me in, you'll *literally* regret it for the rest of your life," said Seamus, using that word we try never to use.

With an effortless hop, Seamus landed beside me, his feet in fifth position.

I pointed to where I was looking, and he followed with his eyes and gasped. Because of course, I wasn't lying. I really was seeing the greatest dancer who ever lived. It was Seamus, reflected in the river's shiny surface.

And now Seamus saw himself, too. He gave a little twirl and looked at his own butt longer than you might have thought possible. He giggled, so pleased. Happy tears flowed down his face, mixing with spray tan until the runoff made him look like a villain that would be "too scary" to be in any Batman film.

But Seamus was so in love with his reflection that he never noticed that I had slipped both sets of the faerie cuffs on his ankles. The pink glow in his feet dimmed.

"Good night, sweet prince," I said, wringing some sweat from my pink wig, then putting it back on. "These should hold you."

"Sorry, did you say something?" said Seamus, who was making bedroom eyes at himself and still didn't notice the ankle cuffs he was trapped in.

"He might never notice, and that's fine," said Captain de Valera as she walked over, spitting out a mouthful of glitter.

"Well done, Boyle," said Tim, giving me the first literal bear hug of my life.

"Well done, Ronan," said Mum as she and Da kissed me on the wig hard enough to leave a bruise underneath.

"Please, please Mum and Da. It's my favorite wig."

Log and Rí slipped in under my armpits to hold me up,

sensing that I was about to collapse, which I was. Not from exhaustion, but from the overwhelming feeling of love. The love of Mum and Da. Whatever was between me and the captain, hero worship or romance or . . . and my undying love of the wolfhounds. Even Seamus's love of Seamus was so strong that it felt like we were all lifted up by our toes a bit.

"I think I have a concussion and I'm going to press charges," hissed Dooley, ruining the moment.

"Did I miss the dancing? How was the dancing?" asked Wee Dave, who cannot see.

"It was amazing," I said. "And quite enough for one lifetime." Captain de Valera pulled out her shenanogram, scanning the sky for leprechaun constellations or anything that might guide us out of this strange place. CYCLOPS EYEBALL-BUTT was rising, but so far off, and partially obscured by purple clouds, that it would be tough to use for navigation.

"Let's move out. It's a long way back to the human realm from here. Wherever *here* even is. And of course, wherever Ireland is," said the captain.

"Is it that far?" I said playfully, like a person with a secret. "Perhaps not. Perhaps it's closer than we know?"

From my sporran, I took out my Roscommon Football Club vastsack and gave it a sassy little twirl.

"Wait . . . you're going to put all of us into your vastsack, and just *walk* us out of the Strangeplace?" said the captain.

"Oh, no, no no. That would be pointless. But . . . right after I kissed NORA the vacuum, I had a little idea. A backup plan in case things went sideways."

"Oh, they went sideways quite some time ago," giggled Log.

"You kissed NORA?" asked the captain, either jealous or disgusted or *let's hope both.*

"I did. Regret the things you don't do, right Yogi Hansra?" I said as my face turned a shade that matched my wig.

And then I let them in on the little secret that was making me giggle: I pulled the model of Lisnacullia out of my vastsack and set it at their feet.

Everyone looked at it, hopeful. A contagious bit of smiling went around.

"You think that will work?" the captain asked,

possibly admiringly. "Going backward through the portcullises?"

"But Ronan, you're the only one who fits. We've been over this. You're so . . . unique in that department," said Yogi Hansra.

"Oh, I know. I thought of that, too. I'm so narrow. I just wish I had thought of this bit before. *You* go in the vast-sack. The vastsack goes in my sporran. *I* go through the portcullis."

"It could work?" giggled Log.

"It has to," I said.

"In a few minutes, we'll either be heroes in Limerick or scrambled eggs over Switzerland," said the captain, smacking me on the kilt in a way that was definitely the football camaraderie version of that.

"Even if it goes wrong, there's no people, bears, wolf-hounds, and wee folk I'd rather be turned into scrambled eggs with," I said, looking at the wonderful faces of our ladyship.

And with a ton of effort, grunts, groans, and clumsy

logistics that I don't have to include in this memoir, a mere forty-two minutes later, I had loaded everyone into my Roscommon Football Club coin purse, along with Dooley and Seamus McSheehy (who never even looked up from his reflection to see what was happening).

I secured the vastsack inside my sporran and lined up my jump toward the model castle.

But before I took the leap, I took a breath. I hadn't had a moment to myself since I could remember, and maybe that was for the best, as it seems that most of my worry, most of my bad feelings about myself, came from my own thoughts. All of me thinking that I am an awkward, narrow klutz who never succeeded at anything—that was the voice in my head. The rest of my ladyship, Mum, Da . . . I think perhaps even Tim—seemed to like whoever I was quite a bit.

Maybe I would try to see myself the way they do a bit more from here on.

I rubbed my bare feet in the warm sand of the Strange-place as I tried to think back on all of the things that got me here, and something happened that made me feel very grown up indeed:

I only remembered the good parts.

And with a little smile that was only for me, I jumped shillelagh-first into a very nice scale model of a castle, and one of two possible endings. Hopefully, it would be the good one, and that's what I will get to remember.

Your friend always,
Ronan Janet Boyle,
Human Republic of Ireland

FROM THE DESK OF FINBAR DOWD
Deputy Commissioner
Special Unit of Tir Na Nog
Collins House, Killarney
Human Republic of Ireland

URGENT UPDATE—NOT CLASSIFIED EVEN ONE BIT

Per Ireland's Freedom of Information Act, I am so happy to inform the readers that Detective Ronan Boyle *did* report back to Collins House. Lord Desmond Dooley is currently awaiting trial in Oifigtown, and Seamus McSheehy has a Netflix Irish Dancing movie coming out quite soon. (Whether it's a movie with a narrative structure, or concert film type thing—I cannot say. Even I am not really sure what the market's desire is for an Irish dancing feature film. Either way, we're all rooting for him here in Killarney. Bon chance!)

Wee Dave with the Courage of a Minotaur and Mary with the Legs that Go On for Days were both awarded the Medal of Useful Shenanigans, which is the highest honor the Special Unit bestows on faerie folk. The Wolfhounds Rí and Lily both received commendations and large bowls of an ice cream called Tuna Sandwich Found on Dashboard, which is a flavor they love. Log MacDougal has been promoted to the rank of detective.

There is nothing in the world that would make me happier than telling you right now that Ronan Boyle was safe as houses, snuggled in his bunk at Collins House. Oh, if only that were the case.

But you and I both know that is not true. From the very beginning, what I've told you is still very much the case. I cannot wish it away, lo though your friend Finbar Dowd has tried. Nor can the Mysterious Doctor Boiko see anything in his magical air fryer that tells the future, and Yogi Hansra is so distraught that her ninety-minute flow class is leaving people hospitalized.

Detective Ronan Boyle is missing. So very missing that it is not even funny. The reward for his person and/or his belt is now up to ten thousand euros, no questions asked.

Here's what we know:

Detective Ronan Boyle left Collins house at 3:17 P.M. seven Wednesdays ago, armed with an NB4 shillelagh and a sentient vacuum cleaner called NORA. Detective Boyle was accompanied by an undercover operative of the Special Unit whose real name is ███████, but sometimes referred to as Horatio Fitzmartin Dromghool.

Thirty-six human hours later, they had violently rescued a far darrig called Pierre from the Undernog mountain range known as The Steeps. Unfortunately, their rescue of this far darrig was so successful that no eyewitnesses were alive afterward to say where Detective Boyle, ██████████ the undercover púca, the vacuum, and Pierre were headed afterward.

We are now just a few more Wednesdays from calling off the search. Is it possible they are all alive and well, having stopped for a bite? Certainly. And until there is evidence to the contrary, or someone turns in his belt for the reward, that is what I, Finbar Dowd, amateur actor and chewing gum vigilante, will choose to imagine.

Please know that if you spot a narrow boy in a kilt accompanied by a far darrig, sentient vacuum, and a donkey/bull/fox/wolf/rabbit/cat/hawk/hedgehog/horse/mule/ladybug in a hat, you are required by Irish law to report them to your local Garda office at once. Failure to do so could result in a seventy-five-euro fine and thirty hours of community service.

I am the person when you have figuratively no one to turn to.

Cautiously optimistic,

F.D., D.C.

ACKNOWLEDGMENTS

These books exist because of Stephanie Rostan and Karl Austen.

These books are excellent because of Maggie Lehrman.

These books are beautiful because of John Hendrix.

Additional thanks to . . .

My friends at Abrams Books and Candle Company: Hallie Patterson, Patricia McNamara O'Neill, Deena Fleming, Amy Vreeland, Jenny Choy, Emily Daluga, and Andrew Smith.

Thanks to my wife, Jenny, and my son, Oliver, who support me even during the writer's block moments when I'm chasing them around the house with an ax. (It's always a goof, I swear.)

Love to my humongous Irish family in Chicago and Ireland: the Lennons, Crowes, Gainers, Dohertys, Lallys—and on my mother's side, the McSheehys, who built Lisnacullia castle in 1420, hoping that one day, a gallowglass warrior of the McSheehy bloodline would use it in an amusing novel.

We did it. It took a while, but we finally did it.

ABOUT THE AUTHOR

THOMAS LENNON is a writer and actor from Oak Park, Illinois. He has written and appeared in many films and television shows, as well as the music video for "Weird Al" Yankovic's "Foil." This is his third novel, after *Ronan Boyle and the Bridge of Riddles* and *Ronan Boyle and the Swamp of Certain Death*.